The Search For The Unicorns

By J P Wagner

Published by Beth Wagner of Moongate Studios dba
Wagner Productions

Table of Contents

Dedication

For Jean, Henry, Lila, Colleen, Al, Don and Lee
Thank you for all of your encouragement and support.

And many thanks to my beta readers
You help was invaluable!

Introduction

Well, the first thing you should know is that this is an unusual undertaking. Normally, you would get an introduction from the author going on a bit about themselves and how they came to be writing this story. You won't get that here. That would be because the author of this book is no longer with us.
Which may cause you to ask, if the author is not around, then how did this book come to be? Will it be the only book published? Did I forget to turn off the stove? (Well, maybe not the last part). I can answer most of those questions, you see I am his daughter and I grew up with him telling stories. Unfortunately, he was unable to see his novels get published. But the last thing he said to me was to protect his books. In my mind that means having the chance to share this novel with you and don't worry, there will be more stories yet to come. This is just the beginning.

- Beth Wagner
Burnaby, BC
July 28th 2018
Introduction

Chapter 1

A MEETING AT THE WIZARD'S HUT

"The Unicorn sang in the summer sun,

With a Right-fol-diddle-ay-day.

The Unicorn sang in the summer sun,

Wet his muzzle and away he run,

And grass grew green where once was none,

With a Right-fol-diddle-ay-day.

"The Unicorn ran where the bank was green

With a Right-fol-diddle-ay-day.

The Unicorn ran where the bank was green,

All silvery grey and fair to be seen

And his favour went to the new young queen;

With a Right-fol-diddle-ay-day."

Carla sang the old song in her clear voice as she sought among the hillside rocks for the plants old Wissagebreht had bidden her fetch. It was a bad year for much of the land. The herbs which had once seemed so commonplace could now only be found in out-of-the-way spots.

She brushed a copper curl back out of her eyes, looking at the telltale little blue flower. Five years of bad harvests in the land had only made the demand for herbs and healing increase. Though Wissagebreht had more and more people coming to him, he didn't appear to be any better off than those around him.

She had asked him about that one evening, after he had gone through a particularly difficult reading-lesson with her. He looked at her. In the way that he always did when he was about to explain something to her which should be obvious.

"With more people being ill these days, what would happen if I asked the prices I did five years back?"

"Why, you would have more money."

"Indeed. And what would I do with more money?"

"Get a larger house?"

"A larger house? For the two of us?"

She looked around the crowded hovel. "For the two of us and all these books and medicines."

"And can you imagine what the people would say when they see us move into a larger house? Keep in mind that all the money we get is earned from their misfortunes."

"Why, they would become envious, of course."

"And worse. Remember young Carticorda, the other night?"

"Yes," said Carla, a little confused about the direction the conversation was taking, "She wanted a spell to put on Fagranda because Carticorda wanted Cordibreht, but he wouldn't look at her so long as Fagranda was around."

"And they believe I might do some such thing if I thought it worth my while. As a result, if they see us becoming rich because they have been sick, they may well come to believe that it is not merely that they have been eating poorly for last years, but that I have also had something to do with the failure of crops and so on."

"And could you do something like that?"

He looked at her with a guarded expression that he always wore when she made inquiries into his powers.

"Whether I could or would do such a thing has little bearing on the case. If they began to think that I were the cause of their misfortune, I would not be safe if I lived in the greatest castle or the smallest hillside hovel. And if I have taught you any wisdom at all over the years, you will not say anything to anyone which might cause them to think about such things."

Carla had learned very early that a conversation which ended like this should not be continued. Even so, Carla felt sure that it would not arouse too much envy for them to have a house in which the winter winds would not whistle throughout it in the dead of night. She and Wissagebreht spent a good deal of time finding and patching cracks, but it seemed that for each one they patched, another appeared.

Occasionally, when she complained too much, he would tell her such things built character. So often that she wished to grow up and go somewhere where she could abandon all pretensions to character.

She sighed. She was coming round to wondering, as she always did when she began to fret over her lot in life, just who and what she was.

She knew that she had been left at the door of Wissagebreht's hut one night many years ago, a mere baby in a wicker basket, warmly but plainly covered.

Who, she wondered, could have left her as a baby for an elderly herb-wizard to take care of? All she could think was that someone had made a mistake. Perhaps they thought that the hovel might contain an old couple willing to take in a child. True enough, Wissagebreht had never indicated that he had been less than willing to take her in, but he was certainly a strange choice for a parent.

The sound of horses' hooves broke into her awareness, and she ceased her song abruptly. As Wissagebreht had taught her, without her fully understanding why, she sat utterly still beside the boulder and waited for the horses to go away. Wissagebreht had taught her for many years that horses meant people of rank, and people of rank were often heedless of the lives or well-being of those of less rank.

As it turned out, however, this group stopped immediately in front of her, and a voice summoned her. As Wissagebreht had also taught her, people of rank tended to be impatient with those who they deemed to be insolent, so she looked up.

The group consisted of two men, brightly dressed, one older and one much younger, both wore swords; three women, all of medium age, looked rather uncomfortable; and five more men in chain armour, who carried long lances, wore swords at their waists and slung shields on their saddlebows. This meant that the group was very important, since only very important people would bring men-at-arms with them. The bright clothes were very costly. Carla could tell this though she had never seen such clothing before, and the youngest man wore something on his head. It looked like a small crown.

She took all this in at a glance as she stood and curtsied nicely and asked, "How may I help you, Milords and Ladies?"

She stood with her head down, waiting for a reply. Wissagebreht had told her that while people of rank felt it rude to stare, they felt it downright insulting for someone of lesser rank to stare at them. Therefore the best way to avoid trouble was to look down.

"We seek the Wizard Wissagebreht. Can you direct us to him?"

This put her into an immediate quandary. While Wissagebreht had always made clear his desire to avoid persons of rank, he had always taught her that persons of rank were not to be trifled with. She saw a frown beginning to gather on the younger man's face, and answered, "Yes, Milord. I am going there myself, if you will follow me."

In a small fit of resentment, she thought to herself, "Let him deal with them, then!"

Off she went, then, running at a fast pace, but one which she knew would not leave her winded and puffing at top of the next hill. She struck the path quickly, then followed it for the rest of the way around a bend. She knew very well that the horses would not be able to come quite so quickly around its bends and twists. Particularly through the willows just before the hut.

She heard shouting behind her as the riders called her to slow down. She went a little faster until finally she crashed through the door. Wissagebreht turned, as he was startled, from something he had been mixing over the stove.

"Lords and Ladies coming this way, right behind me, here to see you!"

"Did they see you?"

"Yes. They asked directions of me."

She felt it strange that that would be his first concern, not that persons of rank were here to see him.

"Ah."

He wiped slender knobbly-knuckled fingers on the front of his apron, then untied the apron, folded it neatly and set it on the table. He looked regretfully at the pot on the stove, then took it off and set it on the floor. “It'll probably be ruined by being taken off the heat too soon, but no help for that."

He walked to the door and opened it, just at the time when the horses had reared to a stamping stop in front of it.

"Good Day, Your Highness, Milord and Ladies."

"Your Highness!" thought Carla, startled. "Whatever is going on?"

She risked a peek around Wissagebreht’s thin frame. The young man with the golden crownlet on his head was frowning. The older man, although he appeared not much less angry, looked a little mystified. There was also another man there, whom she was sure had not been there before. This old man wore grey robes and looked much like Wissagebreht. Though he had a little more meat on his bones. Where had he come from? She was sure he had not been with the group when she had first seen them.

"You know us?" the older and well-dressed man demanded.

"How could I not? His Highness King Bruderic is most recognizable, and Milord Chamberlain Lungand is not much less so. And the Wizard Gaistferu I know at least by reputation. The ladies are Morigrew, Degohi, and Peliso. Do you wish me to name your soldiers as well?"

The young King was instantly curious. "Could you do so? Yes, I see you could. No, we have come not for you to tell us who we are, but for more important reasons. May we get down?"

Wissagebreht's shaggy eyebrows rose. "And if I were so impolite as to say 'No,' what then? Get down, get down, all of you, and come inside. You will have to forgive the state of my lodgings, but we seldom entertain visitors, and practically never noble visitors."

Wissagebreht turned and went back into the hut, leaving the door to swing closed. There were sounds of outrage outside, and a shout, probably from the Chamberlain, for the Wizard to come back. But Wissagebreht ignored them, facing Carla with a look on his face that Carla had never seen before.

"Get back into that corner," he said, pointing at the dark corner where their sleeping-mats were rolled up. "Don't speak and don't move while they're here. And don't ask questions!"

The tone of his voice made her shut her mouth. Swallowing back the question she was about to ask, she scrambled back into the corner, sitting very still and quiet as the Wizard went back to the door.

He swung it open again, almost striking the angry face of the Chamberlain, and demanded "Well, are you coming in?"

Carla could never remember him being so irascible. The lights from the hut flickered in contrast to the gloom of twilight as the ladies and the gentlemen and the Wizard proceeded into the low hut. The men-at-arms tried to follow, but the house was too small for that, so they stayed outside The King seated himself on one of the chairs at the table, and Wissagebreht sat across from him. The others looked around for places to sit, until finally the Wizard got up, pulled out a couple of logs of wood from the pile near the fireplace, and spread a blanket over them. The ladies looked a little distressed about what it would do to their fine clothes, but sat down reluctantly. The Chamberlain looked for a place closer to the King. Failing that, he resigned himself to sitting down beside the ladies.

"Well," said the King, "Since you know all our names, can you say why we have come to see you?"

"Oh, certainly --- "

"Milord King," broke in the Chamberlain. "It is well-known that Wissagebreht was a member of the court before your father's time and left when your father came to the throne. It is not surprising that he should know people from that court, and he may even profess to knowledge of more general matters, but---"

The King frowned. "I know, Chamberlain, that you reject the necessity for this trip, and you have made your objections well-known. With that in mind, will you now allow me to talk to the Wizard?"

Lungand subsided, but his expression said clearly that he was not pleased.

The King turned back to Wissagebreht. "You are a healer, and you gather herbs and plants for medicines, so you will know what the state of the land is in. For the past five years the weather has been bad, and the crops have been progressively worse."

"Yes, I know this."

The King nodded. "Gaistferu," he gestured to the other Wizard, "has been advising us at court, and he tells us that luck of the land is bound up with the unicorns. That the unicorns who always return in the spring have not come back the past five years."

The Chamberlain snorted. The King, without turning his head, said "Lungand, if it distresses you to hear us discuss this matter, you may wait outside with the men-at-arms."

Lungand turned pale, but was silent. The King continued. "Gaistferu says that he does not know enough about this to give advice, but he suggests that you know more, and may be able to help.

"Ah. And no doubt the Lord Chamberlain has made known to you the circumstances in which I left the court? That I served the Old King, before his death and that I waited on the birth of the Queen's child? That one night the Queen disappeared, along with one of her maids, and was never seen again. Though your father said that they were in his care, and he was acting as Regent for the Queen?

"And do you know that I stood against him, denied his right to the rule? And because of that I left the court, coming out here to the wilderness to live by myself?"

The King nodded. "It was never told to me just so, but I know the story. And my father died a year later, when I was a mere babe. Leaving me as the King, with my uncle Lungand ruling for me until I should come of age. Are you then so bitter against us still that you will refuse to help us?"

"I was not bitter against you. I left the Court because I could not condone what was being done, and some will remember that I warned that no good would come of it."

"So it has been said. But will you help us? Tell us what should be done?"

Wissagebreht looked at the young King closely. "Advice I can always give, though the advice is not always welcome. What if my advice were to cost you the crown?"

There was a hoarse sound from Lungand, and even the ladies spoke excitedly to each other. The King turned and looked at them, then turned back to the Wizard. "My people are starving, Wizard. If it were a war against invading armies, I would be expected to risk not merely my crown but my life on their behalf. If it should require that --- "

Wissagebreht waved a knobbly hand. "Not yet, not yet. I merely wished to test where your own feelings lie. And were I to suggest that you give up your crown at this moment, your Chamberlain would have Brehtand and the others in to cut me down in an instant."

"So? What do we do then?"

"Why, we go in search of the unicorns, to see why they have not come back."

Carla saw the Wizard Gaistferu smile at this, a mere twitch of the corners of his lips, then his face straightened.

"I thought you knew that already."

Wissagebreht smiled. "I have a fair idea, but even so it will be necessary to find the unicorns and ask them to come back."

"Then let us go!"

"Not so quick. You must know that the unicorns are shy beasts. Great numbers of people galumphing about on horses are not likely to see much, except a faraway glimmer as the unicorn disappears into the trees. It must be a very small party."

"You have a plan for this, then?"

"Tentatively, yes. We take a very small group about two or three persons, with sufficient provisions, and go off to the usual haunts of the unicorns. Two things must be decided; who shall come along, and what provisions shall we take?"

The King looked at the Wizard keenly. "And I would hazard a guess as to who you will want to come along. Myself is that correct? Leaving the Kingdom in the capable hands of my uncle."

"In fact, my preference would be to take you and your uncle along, leaving the Kingdom in the hands of someone you nominate yourself."

"Milord King, I protest this outrageous behaviour! He presumes to order you about like a small boy! You will not go on any such errand."

"And why not, Milord Lungand? As to his ordering me about, I seem to recall another person who tends to do the same. And I know that despite the information given us by the Wizard at the court, you would never have ridden this way had I not used hunting as a ruse. You have surrounded me since I was a child with people and advisors constantly ready to dissuade me from any course which you thought not proper.

"I am a child no longer, and I will be led by your desires no more. You and I shall go with the Wizard to seek the unicorns and to heal the hurt of our land!"

Lungand stood up and began to protest. The King however, remained seated and he spoke much more mildly, but still firm. "Yes, you have served me well for many years, and you shall no doubt continue to serve me will in this matter."

He turned toward the door. "Brehtand!" he called, "Come here!"

The door opened and one of the men-at-arms burst in. With his sword in hand, he looked frantically around for whatever was endangering his King and Lord.

"There is no danger, worthy Brehtand. I only wish to ask a favour of you."

"A favour, your Highness? You need only to command."

"I know that," said the King, smiling, “But this is a thing, which I would not order, but rather have you do as a favour. The Chamberlain and myself are to go on a trip with this worthy Wizard, Wissagebreht. Whom I would be happy to call friend if he should ever forgive me for the crime committed by my father. The Chamberlain is going to wait here with the Wizard while the others and I return to the city, procure supplies, and come back.

"What I wish is for you to remain here to guard them, keeping them safe from all dangers, until I return.”

"Certainly, your Highness!” replied Brehtand.

"Good.” The King responded. He then turned to the Chamberlain, “Lungand, you will certainly be in no danger here. You may trust me to provide appropriate and sufficient supplies. I hope to return by tomorrow."

He finally turned to Wissagebreht,"I hope this will be sufficient."

Wissagebreht, his face grave, said merely, "You appear to have everything in hand, your Highness."

"Does it truly appear so? I wish—", Bruderic broke off suddenly.

"Enough talk for now. Ladies," he bowed to them and then turned to the Wizard Gaistferu, "And you, Gaistferu, let us go."

With that, they all walked out. The men-at-arms helped ladies mount, while the King sprang into his own saddle. The men looked at Lungand and Brehtand, questioningly, until the King spoke, "And we're off!"

The King spurred his horse into a trot along the twisted path through the willows, leaving the three men looking after him. Carla disobeyed the Wizard's orders and came forward enough to peek around the door to watch the king and his party leave.

As they turned back toward the door, the Chamberlain spoke. "Well, Wizard, do you condemn me? What was I to do? I was not taken fully into my brother's confidence; I have no idea what became of the Queen. I only know that when he died, there were several strong barons who saw an opportunity to do as he had done. To take the crown for their own and I knew that once one did so, the land would be rent with war.

"So I stood up, I spoke to all those who had supported my brother, I put forward his son as the new King, and I declared that I would rule for him until he matured. I convinced most of those who had sworn oaths to his father to confirm those oaths to him. I played one of the barons against another. I built up strength, and I prevented civil war.

"And now many people see all this as merely my way of seizing power, and they sneer behind my back. Wondering how long it will be until my nephew suffers a hunting accident, and I step forward as King in his place."

The Wizard spoke calmly, almost gently. "No, Lungand, I do not condemn you. I only ask you that you search your heart well, and see if you will truly be able to give up power when the time comes. Once that young man reaches the age when you can no longer deny him the rule."

They walked back into the hut, and Carla, seeing them coming, dodged back into the sleeping corner.

The Chamberlain avoided speaking to Wissagebreht, and Brehtand was cautious and wary of them both. So Carla enjoyed watching the three men move around each other for the rest of the day while she remained hidden in various dark corners and other places. She did manage to get near to Wissagebreht once to speak of something which had been on her mind.

"Wissagebreht, that Wizard, Gaistferu, there is something strange about him. I don't trust him."

Wissagebreht nodded gravely. "He is a man pulled in many directions by three things, his ability, his ambition, his fear. His ambition makes him anxious to gain what he feels is his rightful place in the world, his ability makes feel he deserves it, but his fear holds him back.

"He fears to take that one step, that risk, which would very likely win him all he wants. But if it failed, it would lead to disaster.

"Thus he waits, always hoping for that chance to come when time and circumstances will permit him to make his one move, with no risk to himself. And because that time will never come, he will never reach his ambition."

At an early hour of the morning, Carla once more heard sound of horses outside the hut. She peeked outside to the King once more, this time with only ten soldiers and no ladies in his following. There was also a packhorse carrying a large canvas-wrapped pack.

The Chamberlain came to the door and looked out. "Ah, good day to you, your Highness."

"And a good day to you, Lungand. There was some argument as to who should be in charge while we are away, and just how much authority he should have, but we settled that quite amicably. Volkener and Nechtgang share the rule between them, and may only cause to be done those things that they both agree to do."

"They both agree--! Your Highness, those two could not agree between them to take a drink of water if they were dying of thirst!"

"Exactly so. This way, they can neither of them do anything which will be irreparable."

The Chamberlain subsided, but it was clear that he was not particularly happy about this. "We are ready to leave, then?"

I think that perhaps we might wish to change into clothing more suitable for walking. I have brought clothing for you."

"Thank you," said the Chamberlain sardonically.

Wissagebreht looked up at the King. "Your Highness, I hope that you were not intending that this whole crowd should go hunting for unicorns?"

The King laughed. "No, Wissagebreht, that was not my intention. It was only with great difficulty that I was able to avoid bringing more than this along with me, but they are all to wait here until we come back. Only three of us will go hunting unicorns."

"Four."

"Four?"

"Four. I have a young ward around here whom I feel it best to take along with us. Carla!"

Carla came out from where she had been lurking at the corner of the house. Wissagebreht addressed her as though he did not know that she had been listening to almost every word that had been said over the past two days.

"Carla, we are going to seek the unicorns. You, myself, the King, and the Chamberlain. Get yourself ready quickly."

"Yes sir!"

She was turning to go when Brehtand came forward. "Your Highness, where do you go?"

"Why, off into the Great Wild to seek the unicorns."

"And you go alone?"

"No, the Wizard, his ward, and the Chamberlain go with me."

"Milord, you must take a guard!"

"The Wizard has explained that only a small group may go to seek the unicorn, lest they take fright and not allow us near."

"Milord, the dangers of the Great Wild are too well known. Even adding a few more to the party will be a little safer, and probably not that much more frightening to the unicorns."

"Brehtand, I know you speak out of love for me. Nevertheless I must say that this is my final word. No, you shall not go."

"Very well, your Highness." But it was clear that Brehtand was far from pleased.

There was a little more delay while they made preparations. Wissagebreht insisted that while it might be easy on their backs to allow the packhorse to carry everything, it was also the height of folly. "If we lose the horse, we lose everything. No, let us rather each carry a bit of food, a bit of clothing and so on, leaving most of it for the horse, but with us carrying enough that we will not be naked and starving without the horse."

The King scowled, but saw the wisdom of this. Carla, who had been used to doing as Wissagebreht bid without question, simply shrugged and set about making her pack as light as was feasible. She was wondering why the wizard was determined to take her along. It wasn't as though he had not gone away several times and left her to fend for herself for days, even weeks.

She thought to ask him, but with all the people around knew she would get no useful answer out of him. She shrugged. Well, once they were out in the Great Wild she would try to find a chance for the question.

After they had gotten packed up they left. Leaving the men-at-arms sitting and standing uncomfortably around Wissagebreht's hut.

Chapter 2

THE WENDLEASES

For quite a while it was merely a casual walk, for this was all country that Carla knew well as she had roamed practically everywhere. As a chattering child, she walked along side Wissagebreht as he taught her about plants, bushes, flowers and roots. Later on, she had wandered about on her errands to pick particular plants for the old wizard's healing potions.

As they were walking along, Wissagebreht called Carla to him and handed her something. It consisted of a leather patch about the size of her palm, with a long cord, about the length of her arm, tied to each side of it. "A weapon," he said. "It is called a sling, and if you are indeed going to come with us, perhaps you ought to have a weapon. Watch."

He picked up a small round pebble from the ground, and set it in the leather patch. One of the cords had a loop tied at the end of it, and he put that round the forefinger of his right hand. Then, swinging the thing round his head by the ends of the two cords, he let go of the unlooped cord suddenly, and the stone flew rapidly off toward a hillside.

He handed her a small leather pouch. "Pick up suitable stones and put them in this. Practice with it as you go along. It will be hard at first, but it will get easier as time goes on.

Eventually they went up over a small hill. When they went down the other side the land was less familiar and by the time they had gone over the next hill Carla was sure that she had never seen this country before. Carla began to feel uneasy. Without realizing what she was doing, she moved a little nearer to the old Wizard.

He turned, smiling at her. "Afraid?"

"Yes. This isn't home anymore."

"No, it isn't. But this time I don't think it would be entirely safe for you to remain at home. Don't worry my dear. There is some danger in this, but I will try not to let anything happen to us."

They continued to march for some time, then stopped for a rest and a bit of lunch which consisted of some biscuits that Carla had baked before they left and cheese which they felt would be best to bring along rather than to let spoil while they were away. During the march, Carla began to practice with her sling. They stopped to rest twice in the afternoon before the evening. When the sun began to go down, Wissagebreht announced, "We had best look for a place to camp."

They camped in the lee of a hill, making a small fire to do their cooking. The pack-pony was unloaded, and his legs were hobbled so that he could move around and graze on the grass, but could not go too far. Having eaten, they sat around the fire telling stories and singing songs.

Carla sang her Unicorn song, and was astounded at the reactions. Wissagebreht, who seldom expressed an opinion on anything unless pressed, simply smiled slightly. The young King laughed with delight, but the Chamberlain looked as though he would burst with rage. For the life of her, Carla could not see what had caused him to be so angry.

Bruderic smiled, then began a piece of his own:

"They came to the Duke at the dawning of day,

'The Swartings are on us, they rob and they slay,

Our homes are all burning; our families are dead,

On the beasts of our pastures the Swartings have fed!'

He has called for his sword to be sheathed at his side,

His warhorse is saddled; his bold men will ride.

For the goblins are coming, their armies draw near,

There is no longer time for foreboding or fear.

'O Master, dear Master, our hosts are too few!

The men from the Northdale are brave men and true,

And swift though they come they will not come today,

Go not forth till tomorrow; I beg you, Lord, stay!"

But the Duke felt honour-bound to ride at once to the rescue of his people. He went with his small force and attacked the goblins. He was victorious at first. But the King of the goblins rallied his own forces and returned to the attack, eventually overwhelming the Duke and his men. The last of them died in a ring around their mortally wounded Duke. The rest of the Duke's army arrived only in time to take revenge by destroying the whole goblin-host.

It was a long poem and a bit tedious. But as Carla was watching Bruderic, she saw that he was enjoying himself so much that she enjoyed it, too.

Wissagebreht favoured them with a short tale about the Elves. But the Chamberlain seemed to be in a foul mood, and did not try to add anything to the night's entertainment.

Shortly they went to sleep and it seemed to Carla that even more shortly the Wizard was waking everyone up.

The next day was much like the first; save for the fact that this time nothing was familiar. The hills looked similar but once the party rounded them Carla always found something different such as new trees and flowers, many that she'd never seen before. By lunchtime Carla became used to the sensation and she no longer had the desire to run back home to the hut and hide.

The Chamberlain continued in his bad mood, accepting the food offered him with bad grace, and earning from the King an irritated glance. After lunch, Wissagebreht spoke to him.

"Milord Chamberlain, would you walk with me? We have things to speak of." Lungand looked at him and grunted. Then he handed the pack-pony's lead-rope to the King and strode up to walk beside the Wizard. Carla allowed herself to drop back; knowing that the two would wish to talk privately. But she heard the first words, which made her extremely curious.

"Lungand, you do not favour this expedition, do you?"

"No, and I know too well why you arranged so that I should come along. You fear that if I were left behind, I would begin making plans to usurp the throne from that young man back there."

"You think that?" Wissagebreht was surprised. "No, Milord, that was not my reason. But I have a strong suspicion that you doubt the tale of the unicorns, and that you are even more chary of what tale we might return with. I felt it best that you should come along with us the whole way. To see with your own eyes and to hear with your own ears what we see and hear. So that when we return, you will not fear any plot among us."

Suddenly Wissagebreht looked back, frowning. Carla felt herself turning red, and slowed her steps so that she fell further behind. She could no longer hear anything from the two in front save a murmur of voices.

She began to practice with her sling once more. During the first day, she had managed to become skilled enough that she could send the stone off in the direction she intended. Though not far or accurately. She now began picking out marks to throw at, a willow stump, a boulder, or some such thing. The skill seemed to be beyond her, but she was determined to keep trying.

Later on, as the day was passing on into evening, the party mounted towards the crest of a hill. Wissagebreht had rode ahead to scout their path ahead. Suddenly, the Wizard stopped. He then motioned for the rest of the party, who were behind him, to stop as well. Slowly he lay down, then motioned for them to come up, whispering as he did so, "Come up, but carefully, and don't let your head be seen above the hill!"

Carefully, they crept their way up slowly, until they were beside the wizard. Carla was burning with curiosity. Following Wissagebreht's instructions, she cautiously peeked over the hill but kept low to the grass.

Far away on the horizon was a long string of wagons moving across their path. Each wagon had what appeared to be a cover of some sort of cloth stretched over a wooden frame which gave it something of the appearance of a small house on wheels. Carla heard the Chamberlain mutter something that sounded like a curse, then he continued to mutter, "Wendleases! Unpredictable murdering savages!"

Carla continued to watch the wagons, each hauled by teams of two to six oxen with long horns. Wissagebreht answered the Chamberlain. "Say you so, Lungand? Actually, they are people with a particular way of life. And, finding themselves distrusted by other peoples, hold themselves apart from other peoples. And yes indeed, there are some, even some whole tribes, who set upon and kill any they find in their path, but this ought not to condemn the whole race, just as some murderers among our own folk are not taken to condemn our whole race."

Carla could make out young boys and men afoot and riding horses beside the wagons. While at the rear of the whole train was a huge mob of cattle and horses, stirring up a tremendous cloud of dust. They walked in a large semicircle around them and pushed them on, preventing any of them from straying.

The King asked, "What sort of people are they?"

Wissagebreht answered, "They are of many sorts. In fact, the various tribes of Wendleases among them speak about ten different languages. There is even one tribe which speaks a language much like ours. As for this particular band, the tribal symbols painted on their wagons are unfamiliar to me. And I would not wish us to come to their attention, since it is not certain how they might receive us. Let us rest here until they have gone by."

They sat quietly in the lee of the hill. Occasionally, someone in the party would slowly peek over to see whether the Wendleases had completely passed by. At one point Lungand asked, "Are we safe even here? When they move, do they not have scouts and outriders around to seek out enemies?"

"Yes, they will have scouts and outriders, but I think we are beyond the range of such. Best we wait here till they pass."

Finally, after the wagons had gone by and disappeared into the distance, the little band went on. The day passed uneventfully, as did the night.

Again the next day they marched, with nothing to disturb them save the occasional sighting of prairie deer, the skittering of gophers, and the very shy skvaders which would take flight from the nearby brush as they walked. Evening came, and once more, they stopped. They made a small fire for cooking and then wrapped up to sleep for the night.

Again they talked, telling stories and singing songs, as the fire died. As the last coals were still shining, Wissagebreht suddenly held up his hand and said, "Hush!"

"What?" The Chamberlain looked up sharply.

"I heard something out there," Wissagebreht replied.

"Only the horse wandering." Posited the Chamberlain.

"I think not," the Wizard was looking around into the dark. He stood up. Looking around again, he gave a shout, then pointed at the remains of the fire. There was a bang and a burst of flame that blinded them all, and when they could see again, he was gone.

Shouting broke out in the darkness around them. The King and the Chamberlain looked around, groping for their swords. Then men came out into the light of the last coals of the fire. Most of them carried short bows that curved back at the tips. All of the bows had arrows on the strings, and the arrows were pointed at the three. The men were all similarly dressed, in leather trousers and tunic, though some also had a cap of leather which came to a point above the forehead, with long flaps on the sides in front of the ears.

They had all been temporarily blinded by the flash which Wissagebreht had made, but their vision was obviously coming back.

They were all grinning, but there was no good humour in grins, only pleasure at having taken the prey. Carla noticed that they all had scars on their left cheeks. Some of them had scars in a tic-tac-toe pattern. Others had a strange sort of spiral.

The leader was a wizened little man, dressed the same as others, but carrying a rod of twisted black wood in his right hand. He was extremely cheerful at having taken them.

"Oho, Oho, we've taken three of them!"

His accent was a little strange, but there was no mistaking the glee in it.

"All but the wizard, and of course wizards are chancy companions, aren't they? No, no, don't try to draw swords. My men will turn you into pincushions before they are half out of the scabbards."

Lungand looked around, muttered something, and let go of his sword. However, Bruderic held his sword hilt until men with ropes came, roughly grasped his hands, and bound them behind him, while yet another man took the sword. Carla winced at the tightness of her bonds. She would have cried except that she knew that that would only make her captors laugh. She decided not to give them so much satisfaction.

The wizened little leader of their captors capered around, dancing from one person to another as he looked at them carefully. He picked up the packs and sorted through the contents. All the time he chuckled to himself and occasionally spoke to the captives.

"Oho, oho, not rich travellers, are they? But they do have a few things we can use. And as for themselves, well... The girl will make a slave, if only to help the women around the wagons. The boy may make a slave too, if he can be taught to accept his new station. The old one, well he can be our amusement for the night.

"Come, come, quickly, pack up the horse as well. Let us get back to our wagons and think about all this over our beer. Are we ready yet? Hurry, hurry!"

He was such a pest that Carla could hardly believe that the men who were actually doing the work would not eventually tell him to go away. But they seemed afraid of him. When he came too close they stiffened a bit. It was as though they were not quite sure what he might do, but knew that it would be something cruel.

"Come, come, let us go! We are all ready? Good! Prisoners in the middle, lest they should decide to risk running off with bound hands. Now, prisoners, watch the people ahead of you! If any of you stray more than two paces from their path, the people following you will shoot arrows into you. First into your legs and, if you keep going, into your back. Do you understand? Good, then let us be on our way."

They set out then, at a rather fast pace. Carla was surprised to discover just how hard it was to walk with arms bound. Her balance was out, and she stumbled on things that she never thought to stumble on. The two men in front of her were shorter than the rest, with yellowish skin and strangely shaped eyes. They also spoke to each other in some strange language which she did not understand at all.

Occasionally they would laugh a little, a laugh which made her shudder.

They marched thus for about an hour, and Carla wondered every once in a while where Wissagebreht had gone. Despite what the leader of the Wendleases had said, it was not like him to desert his companions when trouble threatened.

Most of her time was spent in trying to keep her balance and in heeding the old Wendleas' warning about straying from the path of those in front of her. Eventually, far in front of them, she could see a small glimmer of a far-off fire, and guessed that that was where they were headed.

Sure enough, it was not much longer before they could see the looming shapes of several wagons, and could hear the barking of dogs and the lowing of cattle. Then, worn and weary and discouraged, they stumbled into the firelight within the circle of wagons. The wagons were old and hard-used. The wagons seemed to have been repaired. But these repairs seemed to be hastily made without any sign of craftsmanship, by the hands of people who cared only that they serve for a little more time.

There were a half-dozen or more women standing around the fire too. When Carla looked at them, she remembered the old Wendleas suggesting that she should be a slave for them, she could not help but shudder. The old leader himself came into the circle and looked around. "Oh, for shame, let us remember our manners and offer a seat to our guests. Quickly, quickly. And we will want our beer too, so see to it, women."

He did not even look at the women as he addressed them, and Carla shuddered again. He treated them as animals. Maybe on the level of the oxen that drew the wagons. Although from the look of them, they had learned not to protest against that treatment. But that only meant that they would be likely to use her, their slave, to take out all their resentment.

Once again she held back from crying, knowing that that would only make her treatment that much the worse.

They were roughly pulled and pushed over to one of the wagons where they were pushed down roughly. Then ropes were put round their necks and fastened to the wagon wheel. The Wendleases all went then to toss another log on the fire and began drinking.

As this was going on a woman approached the captives. She was a young woman with long dark hair, a smooth round face and pointed chin. She carried a water-flask in her hand and bent down quickly, offering it to Carla. "Here, drink. The waiting will be bad enough without the thirst. It is little enough I can do for you."

Carla drank gratefully then, as the young woman passed on to the King, she asked, "Could you not cut our ropes and let us go?"

The woman frowned. "If I am seen doing this much for you, I will surely be punished; if I should do more, what then?"

By this time, she was looking back over her shoulder to see if anyone had noticed what she was up to.

She finished giving drink to the captives, then straightened up and hurried away. Carla wondered about her. There was someone in this group, hard and cruel as they were, who was still capable of showing kindness. However little it may be.

She had little doubt as to how the night would go. Once the men had drunk sufficiently, they would turn to the prisoners and begin to torment them. It was true that they would think to save Carla and Bruderic for slaves. But the thought could easily get lost as the night went on.

Then one of the men got up and began walking in their direction. As he came, he lifted a sort of tarred leather bowl to his lips and drained it. As he took the cup down from his mouth, his eyes changed. His mouth opened as though he were trying to say something, then he fell face-down into the grass.

Another man came over, looked down at his prostrate comrade, and then began laughing. He prodded him with a toe, then bent over and took his shoulder. Suddenly, he too crumpled to the ground.

Carla was beginning to wonder, since the men had hardly had the time to drink enough beer to make them so drunk. She looked around. Other men were falling, or if they were seated, slumping sidewise. The women, most of whom had not been drinking, stood looking at this spectacle, wondering.

Carla looked around for the wizened little man. She saw him looking around at his men who were dropping to the ground like puppets with cut strings. He dropped his own cup, then looked over at Carla, still tied to the wagon wheel. "A witch!" He shouted. "A witch! She has bewitched them all!"

He continued shouting. But his shouting was now in some strange language He groped around for his wand. Then hurled himself to his feet and began staggering toward her.

The campfire flared up in a flash, and the old Wenleas stopped, staring stupidly at it. Out of the flash stepped Wissagebreht. He looked extremely calm, as though this were a thing he did every day. The old leader of the Wendleases stopped gaping and began to raise his wand. But Wissagebreht raised his staff and seemed only to tap him on the temple He fell sprawling to the ground.

The women stood staring, fearful, not daring to interfere. After a sweeping glance at them, Wissagebreht went to Carla. Taking a sharp knife from his belt, he cut her free. He handed her the knife, but she found that her hands were all pins and needles and would not work properly. He smiled, setting the knife down.

"When you can make your hands work again, set the others free. There are things we must do."

Carla wiggled her fingers to get some feeling back into them. Meanwhile, Wissagebreht walked back to the leader of the Wendleases and rolled him over twice. Leaving the black wand lying by itself on the grass. He was careful not to touch it.

Chamberlain spoke. "What magic did you use on them?"

The wizard looked around at the group of women. "No magic, only a little something added to the beer. Indeed, even Carla could show you one or two plants which, when added to drink or food, would give this effect."

Lungand went on to something else that was on his mind. "Why did you flee when they first came?"

Wissagebreht shrugged. "Had I stayed and attempted to fight, we would all have been killed at once. I thought it best to escape at once and come back to rescue you later."

"And if they had simply decided to murder us all on the spot? Or if they had gotten tired of leading us across the plain and decided to kill us somewhere along the way?"

"And if your mother had had four legs, she would have been a table. Lungand, there are risks in anything."

The Chamberlain lapsed into silence, and now Carla was able to cut the ropes on him and the King. Wissagebreht called her, and pointed to the black wand on the ground. "Get some sticks of firewood and pile them on that, being careful not to touch it yourself."

She did as the Wizard said. Wissagebreht kept his eye on the women, lest any of them begin to fear too much what might happen to them and try to attack the small band. A few of the women, those had had a bit more of the beer than the others, were falling to the ground unconscious. While others merely stood dumbly.

After she had piled the wood over the wand, Wissagebreht glanced down and said, "Good enough. Now take a brand from fire and light that. Do not try to light the wand itself, only the wood over it."

She continued to follow his instructions. She also watched Lungand and Bruderic. Who had now regained some feeling in their own hands, and were looking on in wonder. The fire held readily to the wood and she watched as it began to blaze.

"Stand back!" Wissagebreht said sharply.

Surprised, she leaped backward as he pointed a hand down at the fire. Again, there was a bang and a flash and the fire blazed up fiercely.

Carla looked into the heart of the fire and saw that the black wand was burning now. Burning slowly, as though it fought the flames at every step.

Wissagebreht moved, and Carla looked up again. Lungand found his sword and was moving purposefully toward the prostrate leader of the Wendleases. "No, Lungand."

"NO?" There was outrage in the voice.

"In battle, yes, In the heat of anger, yes, but to kill an enemy who lies helpless before you?"

"Helpless for the moment. But what of tomorrow when they come hunting us?"

“Most of them will be too sick tomorrow, possibly the next day, to bother with pursuing us. And as this wand is being destroyed, so is the power that the warlock had over them. They will be a time sorting that out, I think."

"And I say that they are evil, and we would be best to exterminate the lot of them."

"They have been deep in evil, indeed. You see the marks on their cheeks? They are all outcasts. Cast out of the various tribes of the Wendleases, come together in this band for company and for the need to survive. It has been the warlock who led them into evil, for the most part, though doubtless there are many who needed little leading.

"But with the power of the warlock gone, they will perforce seek a new leader, and if the new leader is a better then it will be the better for them. And I seriously doubt that they will take the time to follow us. They have their cattle to consider, the grazing and all. And they travel in a direction different from the one we take. Even revenge will not be sufficient to force them to put their herds into danger."

In all this discussion, Bruderic had stood quietly by, saying nothing. Now, however, he spoke. "Lungand, I think he is right. Better we be gone from here with all speed rather than indulge in our own revenge. Let us go."

They took their packs, hunted out whatever of their belongings they could, took the packhorse, and were on their way.

As they marched, Lungand spoke to Wissagebreht, heedless of who might hear. "Well, this is proof, if proof were needed, that this is too dangerous. The King must go back."

"Lungand, anything is dangerous. If he sits back in the palace forever, there is still the danger that sickness will take him away. In fact, there may even be a certainty of that, for if this quest fails, the land will steadily become less and less productive, until even the richest will have no food, for there will be none to buy. And when that happens what safety will there be in being King in the palace?"

"I did not raise the boy and fight his enemies for this!"

"No, that I doubt not. Yet what other choice is there? The quest cannot be achieved without the King being present, and if the quest fails, so will the land. Did you raise him to turn aside from his responsibilities?"

"No, but --- "

"Then tell me if you can see another choice in all this. If you cannot, then we must continue as we have been, perhaps with more care. But we must continue."

After they had gone some distance from the Wendleases camp, Wissagebreht called them to a halt. "We have to have some rest, whatever else might happen. We will stop here for a time."

Lungand looked up sharply. "And if they come after us?"

"And if we keep going until we are too weary to stand properly? Let us rest, with one keeping watch, for what remains of the night. In the morning we will go on, and get ourselves as far as may be from here."

The Chamberlain did not like this, but he saw the wisdom of it. Wissagebreht took the first watch and Bruderic the second, then they marched again. Despite the Wizard's assurances, Lungand kept looking back over his shoulder for the whole day as though he expected to see all the Wendleases coming in hot pursuit.

They never saw that band of Wendleases again. As they wandered through the plains however, they would occasionally, from great distances, see other bands of Wendleases. But when they did so, they took precautions.

Chapter 3

LOTHBOSC

Several days later they came to a forest. They had seen it for several days as they approached it. First from hilltops as a dark line on the horizon. Then as a long irregular dark patch which lay across their path, and finally as a forest. Dark, green, and faintly ominous.

At last, they stood on a long slope which led down to the first low bushes and beyond them, to the trees. "Now," said Wissagebreht, "we have a choice to make. Our destination is beyond the wood, and we must either go through it or around it."

The King spoke, "From the way you say that, it is obvious that to go through the wood is not so simple as it sounds."

"Not at all. This is Lothbosc, the Wood of Ill Omen. There are rumoured to be various creatures in it which bear little love for men. It is also known that Dark Elves live here, Elves who hate men. It is even said that the wood itself has become imbued with evil, that it knows and detests the tread of men", answered Wissagebreht.

"So we ought to go around?",asked The King as he strained to look into the wood.

Wissagebreht looked sternly at the King, "That is to be decided. To go around will certainly mean a delay in our journey, and we will have to decide just how much of a delay we can afford"

"From all you say, it is not a place for people to enter lightly."

"No, it is not."

"And yet, to go around is to lose precious time. I think we should go on through."

The Chamberlain broke in at this point, "Wizard, it is clear that you know more of this wood than any of us. Why do you not decide, and then tell us what you have decided?"

Wissagebreht smiled. "Perhaps it is because I fear the accusations which would be levelled if I led you into difficulties. There are dangers in the wood, to be sure, but we must not waste time. I hope that if we travel carefully enough, we can pass through unseen and unnoticed by the worst of the dangers."

"How long to go through?" asked Lungand.

"A day and a night and part of the next day."

Lungand rubbed his chin. "And all this time, evil things will be seeking us out?"

Wissagebreht shrugged. "Perhaps, perhaps not."

"Have you gone through this wood yourself?"

"I have been in it a time or two."

"And did you have any difficulties yourself?"

"None that I could not overcome, clearly, since I am here with you now."

Lungand did not smile at the humour. "Let us go, then, as quickly as possible. If it must be done, it would be best to do it with all speed."

Wissagebreht bowed slightly. “If we are all in agreement, then?"

At first, the wood seemed a wood like any other. There were tall coniferous trees. And where the trees let the light through, an underbrush of varying degrees of thickness grew. There were paths as well on which there were animal tracks which were made by natural animals, such as deer and coyotes. Birds twittered and chirped in the branches which lined the paths.

Carla clutched her sling. With constant practice over the last days, she had achieved a reasonable standard of accuracy. Though she was not as consistent as she would have liked.

As they went deeper, the forest grew darker. Light was less able to penetrate to the forest floor, and this in turn meant that less and less underbrush grew. Gradually, there seemed to be fewer and fewer birds in the trees. While on the paths, mixed with tracks of ordinary animals such as squirrels and bears, there were tracks which were unrecognizable.

A feeling grew on them, seeming to grow out of the forest all around. A feeling that they did not belong there. That there was something watching their movements. Something which did not approve of them. Unconsciously, they moved closer together as they walked. It was as though to draw strength from each other to fight off the antipathy of the forest.

The threatening quiet of the forest began to bother Carla. She walked quietly behind Wissagebreht until she could no longer stand it. Finally she burst out, "The forest hates us! It would kill us if it could!"

Wissagebreht turned and spoke soothingly to her. "Yes, I feel it too, and so do the others. The forest cannot harm us by itself. That is for the creatures that inhabit it. Because of that, we must go quietly when we go."

Carla quieted herself. When they started again, she concentrated on watching the Wizard's back. There was a little flaw in the cloth of his garment just above the right hip. By staring at that, she could avoid allowing the feeling of the forest to bother her so badly.

Night came early. While it was high in the sky, the sun could penetrate occasionally to the forest floor. The sun had declined toward the horizon. However, its rays no longer reached the travellers, and shortly the trail became harder and harder to follow.

Wissagebreht finally turned to the others. "I wish we could go on, but the light fails too fast. We must camp for the night."

As they made their preparations, Wissagebreht cautioned them against going far from the group. He also insisted on gathering as much firewood as could be found. "Tonight," he said, "we will want to keep a fire burning at all times. It will not protect us against everything, but it will protect us against some things."

Carla shuddered. She had never known Wissagebreht to express his fear so openly before. What kinds of things could be in this wood that would make him so careful? Bruderic saw her concern and came over to where she was gathering firewood. As he picked up some sticks, he said, "You worry too much."

"I worry? What concerns me is the way he worries." She pointed her chin toward the Wizard, who was busy with the preparations for supper, "I have never seen him so worried, and when he is afraid, I become terrified."

Bruderic nodded. "You have lived with him a long while, then?"

"Since I was a babe."

"How did that come about?" Bruderic let his curiosity overwhelm his good manners.

Carla shrugged. "All I know is that I was left on his doorstep in a basket, and he has raised me since. I have asked him occasionally if he knew who my parents were, but he always manages to change the subject."

"That would be hard, to not know who your parents were, nor why they would choose to leave you alone at the door of a wizard's hut."

"Oh, sometimes it isn't so bad. I use my imagination to pretend that my mother was a great lady who had to leave me for some reason. And that eventually, she will find me and bring me back to her castle."

A thought struck her. "You have no parents either, do you?"

“Oh, but I know who they were. my father became King when the old King died. Some people claim that he killed the King, but that is a lie, for the King died after a fall from his horse. My father merely made himself Regent for the Queen, and fought the Barons who would have overthrown her."

“I see,” Carla was quiet.

She knew enough about the stories and suspicions which had surrounded Bruderic's father. She was sure that speaking of those things at all would upset the young man.

Bruderic picked up a dry stick and struck it suddenly against a tree root so that it snapped in two, "They tell so many stories about the evil things that my father did! My uncle says that many of the stories are told out of envy and many out of ignorance. But even he cannot always tell me that they are false. He tells me that I must be the King. That I must rule the land and not allow anyone to say that I have no right.

"But I hear people talk when they don't know I'm listening. So many of them hate me for my father's and for my uncle's sake. I often wish that the Queen's child would come back and prove his identity and take this burden from me!"

Carla didn't know what to say, so she looked away and picked up another stick.

"Maybe," she said tentatively, "Maybe when you grow up you could give up being King, go do something else?"

Bruderic laughed, a bitter little laugh, "I said as much to Lungand one day after I had had to watch justice being done on a group of people who had been saying that I was not the rightful King. When we were alone, I told him that when I grew up I would give up the throne and be King no longer, if this was what it meant.

"Lungand looked at me and said, 'Bruderic, if it distressed you to see those men die today, think what it would mean if you give up the throne. I can name you five men now. Indeed, you could name them yourself if you thought of it. Those who would immediately try to set themselves up in your place. It would mean war and battle with hundreds or thousands being killed, rather than three or four. And it is only by being King, by showing that you will allow no one to challenge your rule, that you prevent that.'"

He was quiet again for a while, then he spoke, "So here I am, a King that few of my subjects like, and I dare not think of giving it up for fear of what that would mean my people. It is not a position I enjoy."

Carla didn't know what to say to that. Fortunately, she was spared the necessity of saying anything by Wissagebreht's calling them to come in with the wood.

A little later Carla had a chance to talk to Wissagebreht alone, "Did you know that the King doesn't like being King? Everybody hates him, and they tell all kinds of wicked stories about his father."

The Wizard nodded, "His father was a strong-minded man who saw his chance to become King and took it. As for the Queen, she was in his care, she and her maid. And the 'care' was little more than comfortable imprisonment. One day it was announced that the Queen, while ill with plague, had died after giving birth to a child. The child died soon after. Shortly after that, the Regent began to call himself King.

"It was irony indeed when he himself died in a fall from a horse when Bruderic was only a babe. His brother Lungand, fearing what would happen to the Kingdom, declared himself Regent in his nephew's name. I suppose he thought it better to have a King of doubtful legitimacy than have all the powerful men of the Kingdom fighting for the crown."

"But what of the Queen, Wissagebreht? What really happened to her and her child? Could they not come forward sometime and demand the throne?"

"Here, go cut up these carrots into the pan there; we will have a stew for our supper."

As she moved off to do his bidding, Carla realized this was the same sort of thing he had always done when she had asked about her parents. This was clearly something else he did not wish her to know, but why?

But Wissagebreht began to tell them all a long tale out of the Elven Kingdoms, and soon she had forgotten her questions. The thought came back to her, however, just before she went to bed. So she went to the Wizard and spoke to him quietly, "Wissagebreht, who am I? You have never told me; you have always changed the subject. But I know that you know. If you did not, you would have told me at least that. Now I want to know who my parents were."

Wissagebreht looked at her, frowning a little. The frown suddenly disappeared to be replaced by a smile, "At this time and this place you would insist on knowing who you are? Carla, there were many reasons why I never told you before, and there are reasons why I would not tell you now. However, if you will agree to wait, I will promise to tell you when this quest is over and we are safe home.
"I promise you, there is a good reason why I would prefer not to tell you now. With that in mind, can you agree to wait?"

Carla looked at him. For a moment she wanted to be stubborn, to insist that he tell her now. But she knew that he always had good reasons for what he did. A little reluctantly, she nodded her head.

Each of them took a turn that night sitting up beside the fire and keeping it burning. Wissagebreht gave them a stern injunction before bedtime. "The fire must be kept burning. But be careful about using up all the wood. If the wood is used up before the night is over, we may find ourselves in trouble. It will not be wise for anyone to go searching for wood in the darkness."

Wissagebreht took the first watch, and woke Bruderic for the next watch. Bruderic woke Carla, and Carla in her turn woke Lungand. Nothing bothered them in the night. Even so, Carla had the feeling that there were things out there beyond the light of the fire. Things that feared the fire only a little more than they hated the presence of the four travellers. Once or twice she thought she caught the gleam of eyes in the darkness. But the gleam disappeared so quickly that she could not be sure that she had really seen it.

After she had woken the Chamberlain, Carla snuggled back down into her bed to sleep. It seemed only a moment later that she was woken up by something. She came up out of sleep with the feeling that she had had a terrible nightmare. A nightmare she could not remember.

She sat up and looked around. The others were awake too, and looking around as well. Had they had nightmares too? A moment later the Chamberlain pointed off at something approaching through the woods. At first Carla could make out nothing but a sort of moving glow, then the shape was clearer.

It was coming along the trail that they had followed, and it seemed to be shaped like a man. It had two arms and two legs, and in its right hand it clutched a double-headed axe. Its face had two large eyes, a large grinning mouth, and a short stubby nose. it wore no clothing, and its flesh was red and glowing as an ember from the fire. From its back, shoulders, and trunk protruded long, sharp quills. It suddenly saw them and began to hurry forward. A feeling of dread and despair seemed to leap out from it to touch all the travellers.

Wissagebreht came to his feet and raised his staff. "A Spiny Demon!" he muttered, "A Bhalgon!"

"Can we fight it?" asked Bruderic.

Wissagebreht turned a tight little smile on him, "Will we have any choice but to fight it? No, Bruderic, I think this is for me. The rest of you stand well back, for all you could accomplish is to harm yourselves and hinder me."

Bruderic moved back, but he took his sword from the sheath and watched.

The Wizard took a stance between the Bhalgon and the rest of the party and waited. The demon rushed toward him, slowing as he saw that Wissagebreht was not going to move, "Turn back, Child of the Flames! There is no prey for you here!"

The feeling of dread abated for a moment.

The demon stopped a moment, stared at Wissagebreht then leaped against him. Swinging the axe up as he leapt and and bringing it down as he landed. The axe clashed against the wizard's staff. As the demon readied its next blow the wizard took advantage of the opening to strike at the demon's chest. Again and again the demon slashed at the wizard with its axe. But Wissagebreht parried the blows each time, and returned the strokes with his staff. He seemed too light to strike effectively, but with each blow of his staff, the demon shuddered.

Suddenly the staff and the axe were dropped and the two were struggling hand to hand. Bruderic stepped forward and began to raise his sword. But the Chamberlain laid a hand on his shoulder, restraining him. The feeling of dread came over them all now. A despair which weakened the knees and threatened to cast them to the ground. Then Wissagebreht moved. One moment he was holding the demon back and the next he was standing erect, holding the demon above his head. With hardly a pause he threw the demon down.

The ground shook, flames leaped up, and Wissagebreht staggered back. There was a hole in the ground, and fire still came from it along with horrible shrieking noises. The Wizard, his face pale and strained, said to the others, "Quickly, gather up what we can and let us leave this place! This battle will have awakened most of the forest, and I think we can no longer hope for our passage to go unmarked."

They frantically tossed their belongings into their bags. Then hurriedly packed the pony. Finally, they were on their way. Carla had expected them to start out at a run judging by what Wissagebreht had said. But instead they started out at a walk. They had been going for only a few minutes before their pace began to pick up although it never came near to a run.

Carla watched the Wizard forged on ahead of her. She was a little worried for he did not seem to be walking properly. From time to time he seemed to stagger a little, and she knew that he was dreadfully tired. The battle with the demon, short though it was, must have required more strength than it appeared.

On they hurried. Between the large tree trunks. Through the still-dark forest. Eyes and ears alert for any sign that they had been noticed by anything hostile. The belated rays of dawn came through the trees as they hurried on, and at moment Wissagebreht held up a hand, "We have to move quickly, but we will move the quicker for a bit of food in bellies, even if it be only a crust of bread."

As they got out the bread and the water-bottles, Carla surreptitiously eyed the wizard. He showed little sign of weariness, though there was a tightness around his mouth and eyes. "We may not dare to stop again for some time, so carry your bottles ready. Don't drink heavily. Just a sip here and there. Are we ready to move?"

No one answered. Though Carla did consider for a moment suggesting that they should have a longer rest. But before she even opened her mouth to speak, she recalled the demon rushing through the forest toward them. She also thought of other such things out and hunting them. She said nothing.

They were striding through the trees again. Carla was almost gasping for breath as she strove to keep up. Something black flickered overhead. Wissagebreht cast a quick eye up to see what it could be, and seeing a black bird swooping down toward them he said, "Ah! it will not be long now before they are on the track!"

Puffing himself, Lungand asked, "The bird was some sort of scout or messenger? Perhaps we ought to kill it?"

The Wizard shrugged, then called back over his shoulder. "That would serve little purpose. If it did not come back, they would know that there was something to hunt and would be coming for us in any case."

More light was coming through the trees now. Carla tried to convince herself that they were coming into the less hostile parts of the forest. There was little sign of that, however. Except perhaps, for a little snore underbrush, and she knew it was little more than an impression born out of a wish.

On the travellers went. Suddenly, the silence was broken by the sound of a drum pounding. It seemed to be coming faintly, from somewhere far behind them. Carla caught the faint gasp from Wissagebreht, "Well, they are aware of us now, and they will be pursuing. And I fear that they can move faster than we."

"Do we make ready to fight, then?" enquired Bruderic.

"Not yet. We need to get as near to the edge of the forest before we turn at bay. It is even possible that we can get out of the forest before they overtake us. And if we do, then most of the pursuers will not dare to follow."

A little later they stopped for a short rest. They sat against tree-trunks, took a few sips of water and rinsing out their mouths, then they got up and went again. Occasionally, far off behind them they could hear the drums sounding again. The hush of the forest was broken. There seemed to be voices all around them. Voices which spoke just a little too faintly to be distinguished. But voices which were telling the pursuers where their prey was.

"Fortunately," gasped the Wizard, "none of them seem to be in front of us."

"But you fought the demon and won," said Bruderic. "Why should you fear anything else in the wood?"

"Because I have used up much of my strength fighting the demon, and I have no idea how useful I would be in any fight now. And because other things in this forest may attack in other ways. And because you should take my word it that we would be better to flee the forest as quickly as possible."

They had little breath for talking, but instead saved all their energy for walking. At last they came to the point where Carla could be certain that the forest was thinning out. There was more underbrush now. The sun shone more and more frequently through the overspreading leaves and branches. Casting patches of gold on the ground.

But even as she was taking heart from this, the drums sounded behind them. They were closer now, and there was an ominous note to them. She was tired now. So tired that she was sure that she would fall by the trail soon to be taken by whoever or whatever pursued them.

She could see the Wizard in front of her nearly staggering with weariness. She wondered if he would drop before she did. Bruderic came up beside her. "Give me your arm, Carla. Lean on me a little."

She looked at him, then snorted as she saw the weariness in his own white and strained face. "Lean on you?" she gasped. "Then we'd both fall down! I'll manage by myself."

They took another short rest a little later. Again, it was only a short pause for a sip of water, then they were marching again.

Now the forest was less dark and forbidding, but Carla had no idea how much further they had to go. She briefly thought of asking Wissagebreht. But she took one look at him. He was practically staggering with weariness. So she decided not to bother him with questions right now. The drums sounded behind them again. They were closer now. She wondered whether they would get out of the forest before the pursuers caught them.

Even as they went, Carla remembered the Wizard's warning about how some things in the forest might dare to come outside. Would the pursuers dare to come out, and if they did, how far would the little band have to go in order to be safe?

"Come on!" shouted Wisssagebreht, calling somehow on the little strength he had left, as he broke into a run. The rest followed him, running at first with a stagger. Then as they found their balance and their final strength, with more assurance. They were not running swiftly, but they were running.

Light streamed down into the forest now. The tallest of the trees were not very tall, and the brush was thicker beside the trail. Carla was not sure, but she thought she heard behind them the tread of many feet. Suddenly, they were out of the trees and into the brush surrounding the forest proper. But still the Wizard ran. The drums sounded behind them. Sounded nearly at their very heels, and Carla almost jumped forward.

The Wizard pulled off the trail, motioning the others to go on by. Carla went by, heard him snarl at Bruderic, "Go on, you young fool! You could only get in my way!"

The brush was thin and sparse now, and even Carla could see over and beyond most of it. She kept on down the trail until it passed over a small hill. Going up the hill required all the strength she still possessed. When she reached the top, she stumbled and fell. She pushed herself to hands and knees. But the pack on her back seemed to weigh a ton. Even the fear of what came behind them could not give her the necessary strength to gain her feet.

Bruderic leaned down to take her arm and help her up, but her weight was too much for him and he also fell. He rolled over and sat up then stayed there, staring. "Look!" he cried. "The Wizard!"

Carla, still on her hands and knees, managed to turn a little and look back the way they had come. Lungand was pounding along the trail now. But beyond him Wissagebreht stood, his hands raised. His right still held the staff, and he was speaking words in some strange language. They could still not see who or what was pursuing. Save for an occasional dark patch flitting among the trees on the trail beyond the Wizard.

A wind suddenly began to blow from the Wizard into the forest. First in small fitful gusts, then a stronger and steadier breeze, then a rushing wind. The trees and bushes whirled and whipped in the wind. Dust, leaves, and twigs rose from the path and from the forest floor and blew towards the pursuers. Then it was a gale blowing full force, one or two small trees were uprooted and flung back into the wood. It was no longer possible to see any sign of the pursuers.

The wind ceased as suddenly as it had begun. The forest grew still again, and Wissagebreht stood for a moment, then crumpled to the ground.

Lungand stood over Bruderic and Carla. His chest heaving, "We ought to move a little further from here before we stop."

Carla struggled slowly to get to her feet. "We have to get Wissagebreht."

The Chamberlain looked down at her in anger. "We have no time to waste! He has driven them away for a time, but who knows for how long?"

She shook her head stubbornly. "I will not leave him behind."

Bruderic spoke. "She is right, Lungand. We cannot leave without him."

Lungand said nothing further, but it was plain he disapproved. They went down to where the Wizard lay, and Carla went down on one knee beside him. He still breathed, but his eyes were closed and he was dreadfully pale.

She looked up at the others. "We should get a little further from here before we stop."

With Carla and Bruderic on one side and Lungand on the other, they moved Wissagebreht along the trail. They went over the hillock and a little ways further on, then they had to stop. They may have forced their own weary bodies a little further. But they could not have done so supporting the Wizard.

For a little while they lay there panting. With thoughts of nothing but the possibility of falling asleep. Sleeping the rest of the day and the night as well. Carla slowly forced herself to sit up, looking at Wissagebreht. He was still breathing, still dreadfully pale, and he did not look well. She tried to remember any of the things he had taught her, but all she could think of was that he needed food.

How to feed him, though, in his present state? Probably the best thing would be a bit of broth. Come to think of it, the whole lot of them could do with something a little more than the crusts of bread they had gnawed on while they fled the forest.

She looked around. Bruderic was lying on his back, his eyes closed. The Chamberlain, though he was trying hard to stay awake and watchful, was slumping wearily forward. "Bruderic!" She called.

His eyes opened and he looked at her without comprehension.

"Bruderic, make a fire! Just a small one, for some cooking. We have to get some food for Wissagebreht, and the rest of us could stand to eat a little as well."

He stared at her, his eyelids beginning to droop. She reached over and gave him a push. "Come on, wake up! Just make a little fire, then you can sleep all you want!"

He grimaced, gave her a nasty look, but got up and began to get out his fire making apparatus. She turned to her pack and began to get out the things she would need.

Mainly by force, she prevented herself from falling asleep. Sorting out her cooking equipment, she soon had a good little broth bubbling in the pan. Lungand by now had slumped sidewise and was snoring gently on the ground. While Bruderic sat watching her carefully. Wissagebreht continued to lie pale and still.

She filled a cup of broth, then looked at the King. "Get yourself a cup, and have a bit," she said, "You might want some bread with it."

He tore off a piece of bread and took his cup, but Carla was already approaching the Wizard. She lifted his head, held the cup to his lips, and coaxing, he swallowed weakly. After a little urging She set his head back down on her lap and took a sip of broth herself

She eventually managed to get most of a cup of broth into Wissagebreht, though he never fully woke up. There was one final sip left in the cup, but try as she might she could not get him to take it. He had gone so deeply asleep that no amount of talking, shaking, prodding or poking could bring him out of it. She finally shrugged and laid his head down, covering him with a blanket, and got some broth for herself.

She sat beside him, drinking the broth and watching him. She didn't know when she fell asleep. Though there was a point when she began feeling cold and started to wake herself up to do something about it. But, before she could, the cold went away and she dreamt that someone had put a blanket over her.

When she woke it was morning. Wissagebreht was lying there beside her. He was sound asleep but looking much healthier. Lungand was sitting up in his blankets a little ways away. Bruderic was still asleep, but was beginning to stir a bit.

She sat up, and at that movement Bruderic opened his eyes. "Morning again?"

Lungand chuckled a little. "Yes, morning again. And I think it would be best if we see about a little food. The Wizard looks as though he will have recovered somewhat. And if that is so, he will probably want to continue on our journey."

As they set about restarting the fire and getting out the food, Wissagebreht woke. "Ah, then we did indeed survive? Good, good."

He rolled out of his blankets and got to his feet, a little stiffly. "We have been here the whole night, then?"

"Yes," answered the chamberlain. "Everyone was a little too tired to go further."

The Wizard frowned. "I would have preferred to have seen you go on a little further from the wood before camping. But since no harm came of it, so much the better. Now what of food?"

After they had eaten, Lungand asked Wissagebreht, "Well, how much further do we have to go?"

The wizard shrugged. "Not much further, hopefully. Tomorrow, the day after, we should be coming upon them. At that time we will have to be careful so as not to frighten them away."

"Are they really so easily frightened, then?" asked Bruderic.

"Very much so. They might see a man, and even allow him to approach them. But the least little movement which seems too sudden or too threatening will send them fleeing."

They talked a little over their breakfast, then they were on their way again. The pack-pony, fortunately, had not strayed far from where they had all collapsed for the night. Carla noticed that Wissagebreht seemed a little stiff for the first little while. But rapidly, he seemed to recover.

Wissabreht did not, however, keep up the sort of pace he had set previously. In the middle of the morning, they took a lengthy rest. Then at noon they had an even longer one. Once again in the middle of the afternoon he insisted on stopping for a while. He finally called a halt to the travelling early in the evening.

He went to bed early that night and was up late in the morning, but by midday, he seemed to have fully recovered. At their lunch break Lungand asked him, "Do we expect the unicorns to be in a single place, or do we only know that they are somewhere out here?"

Wissagebreht grinned. "I fear it is the latter. We have not done all the walking we will have to do just yet."

Lungand's face began to look a little more serious.
"So we wander around out here looking for unicorns who may or may not be within ten miles of us," he grumbled, “Meanwhile, back in the kingdom, are at least half a dozen men ready and willing to attempt to unseat the King if it seems at all possible."

Wissagebreht smiled slightly. "I did not promise that it would be easy, Lungand. I only promised that there would be a possible solution to the problem in which the land finds itself."

"So we trade the possibility of famine and starvation for the possibility of civil war?"

Wissagebreht shrugged. "The possibility of famine is real. It is waiting for us if we cannot deal with the problem of the unicorns. The problem of the civil war is quite another. And it depends entirely on whether any particular baron or barons feel they have the strength to reach out and seize the crown. Let us deal with what is real right now, and leave the possible problems for the future."

Lungand subsided, muttering.

All that day, remembering the Wizard's suggestion of when and where they might find the unicorns, they walked and watched carefully. They saw grasshoppers hopping in the grass causing it to ripple like a pebble in an ocean of green. They saw butterflies flittering around and landing on nearby bushes or grass. Occasionally an eagle would soar high above them in the vast blue sky. But there were no signs of unicorns that day. They camped that evening beside a spring. The spring fed a small pond which was surrounded by a large stand of willows. The pond then spilled out into a brook which went meandering off across the plain.

Wissagebreht looked around at the spring and its environs and said, "Well, I think that this would be as good a place as any to set up a camp. This will be our base, and from here we will go out and about to see if we can find any unicorns. If we make our camp a little ways from the water, say on that hillside there, why we may find that a unicorn or two will come to us unsought."

Chapter 4

QUICKFOOT

Early the next morning, Carla went down to the spring for a drink. As she was approaching the spring she stepped into a small hole in the ground, stumbled, and fell into the willows. When she tried to stand up again, she found that her right ankle could barely hold her weight.

She looked up at the camp. She knew that if Bruderic saw her limping up the slope he would immediately come dashing down to help her. For some reason the mere thought of that brought her temper to a boil. She had practically reached the campfire before anyone noticed her. By that time, it was too late for anyone to do much besides expressing distress.

Wissagebreht sat her down and checked the ankle, probing it with careful fingers. At last, he looked up and said, "Well, there is no bone broken, but I doubt if you'll be able to walk for a few days."

Carla shrugged, "I suppose I'll Just have to stay round the camp and make sure there are meals for you when you get back." She felt less cheery than she sounded, however, for she had hoped to be able to see a unicorn.

The Wizard looked at her sympathetically. "We'll leave Bruderic here to keep you company."

She sat up straight. "I don't need company! You know I've spent days, even weeks, alone! All of you go off and look for your unicorns! I'll be quite all right here!"

Wissagebreht looked at her sharply. "You're certain you'll be all right?"

"You need to ask that? You taught me how to get along all by myself from an early age. Don't I have everything I need here? And you'll always be coming back in the evening, won't you?"

He nodded, saying nothing. He then got a piece of cloth and wrapped her ankle tightly. "Don't try to move too much or too far. The more rest you give it, the sooner it will heal."

The three went off then, leaving her sitting at the camp. After feeling sorry for herself for a while, Carla decided that she might as well do something useful. She warmed up some water and washed a lot of clothes. Then she hung them up on various sticks which she planted in the earth around the campsite.

Carla spent a lot of time resting and dozing, but there was only so much time that could be spent that way. Towards evening, she decided to get something for supper. Something beside the kinds of hurried meals they had had for the last while. She gathered together bits of dried meats from the travel rations, found some wild herbs and dandelions growing nearby which she combined with some spring water in a pot over the fire. She was practically done with that when the men all came back. They were somewhat tired, hungry, and grumpy. She was glad that she had taken the time and trouble over the meal.

There was little conversation during supper. But afterward Bruderic said, "Thank you for cooking the meal, Carla. You clearly took some time over it."

"Simply being lamed does not make me incapable of helping out. It was the least I could do."

"And it was certainly appreciated," said Wissagebreht.

Lungand simply grunted, but it could be seen that he, too, had appreciated it.

After having eaten, Bruderic went off into the willows. He returned a little later with two poles of medium length, each topped with a fork. Sitting down beside the fire, he carved these two poles down. Thereby producing a pair of reasonable crutches. He even put fastened pegs for her to hold onto, then surveyed his work with no little pride.

Carla realized very early on in the process of Bruderic's crutch-building, what he was about and she was torn. On the one hand, she felt irritated about being reminded of her lameness. But nevertheless, forced herself to act and sound grateful. Carla realized that the next day, when she was trying to hobble around the campsite, she would be grateful indeed. She pushed her irritation into the back of her mind as she said, "Thank you very much, Bruderic. These will be very useful to me."

And she gave him as big a smile as she could manage, without making it clear that she was pretending.

He smiled back. "I hope that they will make some amends for having to stay around the camp all day. At least you will be able to move a little easier."

And his understanding tone made it even harder to abide.

The next morning, the men set about to ensure that the campsite had plenty of water. After the men had gone out, Carla sat around for a while. Time went by and soon she got too restless. She looked over to the crutches. It took a little getting used to, but she managed to move around well enough on the crutches to be able to tidy up the camp.

First Carla heated up some water on the fire and used it to clean up the dishes from breakfast. Then she shook out the bedrolls and folded them neatly away. Once the campsite was tidied, there was little more to do for now so she napped. After she woke up from her nap, she sat for a while singing songs. She then swung around on her crutches exploring, and finally became extremely bored. It was a little after she had eaten lunch. She sat on the hillside watching the spring bubble out and roll down the hill to the pond, when over the hill trotted a unicorn.

She saw him come from the time his head first appeared over the brow of the hill. At first she thought he was merely a deer, come to drink at the spring. But the grey dapple colour was wrong for any deer she had ever known, and there were no antlers, just one horn on the forehead. Suddenly she sat up straight as she soon realized what she saw.

She grabbed for her crutches. Just as she was about to work her way to her feet, the thought came to her. All her thrashing around on crutches would be more likely than not to frighten the beast. She sat still.

The unicorn turned his head toward her, and she felt his surprise, almost as though he had said out loud, "Hello! What are you doing here?" Then he turned back toward the pond and went down to the bank to drink.

Carla felt that she had somehow been studied and considered as no threat. She wondered what to do next. She might offer it food, but what did unicorns eat? And if she stood and tried to make her way to the pond, it might well frighten the beast. On the other hand, if she reported that evening that she had seen a unicorn and had done nothing, what would Wissagebreht say?

The unicorn was drinking, its head down toward the pond. Perhaps now would be the time to get to her feet. When it wouldn't notice the movement so much. She pulled herself to her feet, getting her crutches under her. At that moment, the unicorn threw up its head and looked around at her. Carla froze.

It looked at her for a time, then turned back to the water. She began to make her way slowly down toward it.

She had gone practically no distance at all when it stopped drinking again and turned toward her. Turning its whole body this time.

The liquid blue eyes stared at her, and she had a feeling that they were staring right into her mind. It spoke out loud. "What are you doing here all alone, child?"

She stood still and stared. What little she knew about unicorns did not include the fact that they spoke, or that they spoke readily. While she was staring, the unicorn spoke again.

"Come child, answer me. Why are you all alone out here in the wild?"

Carla managed to overcome her awe to respond, "Why, I am not alone. There are three others with me"

There was laughter in the unicorn's voice. "Are there indeed? Then they must be invisible, for I cannot see them."

"Oh, they have left me here in the camp while they go out searching for unicorns," even as she realized what she had said, the unicorn was answering in a voice full of laughter.

"They have gone off looking for unicorns, have they? And you, left alone in the camp, are the one who has actually found the unicorn. How amusing."

It moved closer to her, its horn gleaming in the summer sunshine. She felt its fierce wildness. The strength of muscles which could, and would, take it bounding away and free from any danger that threatened.

"So why are they searching for unicorns? For one of those magical potions which require the powdered horn of a unicorn, I suppose?"

"Oh no, not that! We merely want to know why the unicorns have not returned to our land. The prosperity and health of the land are bound up with the return of the unicorns, and for five years they have not come. We have come to find out why."

There was a long pause. "Who has come with you, then?"

"The Wizard Wissagebreht, the Chamberlain Lungand, and his Royal Highness, King Bruderic."

"Ah."

"Why have you stopped coming to our land?"

The blue eyes stared at and into her. "Perhaps better that question should be answered once for the whole group of you. When will your companions be back?"

"This evening, toward sundown."

"And I will be back as well, after sundown."

"Do you have a name?"

"I am called Yssagarit Quickfoot," Laughter came into the unicorn's voice again, "And speaking of quick feet, you seem slow on yours. You were injured?"

"Yes, I fell the other day and hurt my ankle."

"I can heal you, if you would like.”

"You can?"

"Oh yes,” Yssagarit was solemn now, “It will not be comfortable, but it will cure you."

She was immediately excited. "Please do so."

Again the eyes looked into her. "Very well, then."

The unicorn bent his head and laid his horn upon her injured ankle. There was a sudden stab of pain — a pain which brought tears to her eyes and caused her to scream aloud. She almost fell, but instead clutched the crutches tightly to keep her balance. The pain passed, gradually, and was replaced by a throbbing. The throbbing began to subside as well, and Carla put a little more weight on the ankle. The pain was gone. All this time Quickfoot was standing, looking at her. She dropped the crutches, standing erect. Quickfoot looked at her and laughed. "I told you that it would not be comfortable, did I not?"

Carla had to cast her mind back, and she did recall that he had indeed told her it would not be comfortable. She, however, had paid little attention to that. Being more concerned about having her ankle healed. She nodded. "Yes, you did. Thank you for the healing."

"For nothing, little maiden. Your ankle is well?"

"Yes," she answered, still a little surprised at it all, “Quite well."

"Good! Sing, then!"

Somewhere in the back of her mind Carla knew that this was a strange request. But the rest of her being felt it completely natural. She began to sing. Slowly at first. Then, making up words as she went along, she sang a song that quickened and seemed to grow of its own accord. As it went, it began to draw her feet into a dance, and her feet began to catch up to the song, and faster. Then the song began to speed up, moving faster and faster until before she knew it, Quickfoot was dancing and gambolling along with her.

His four feet flying as quickly and in more intricate steps than her two. From his mouth there came a whistling which matched the song she was singing. They danced and pranced there in the sun for a long time. The song did not slow, it merely stopped suddenly. Carla tumbled in a heap on the ground. She was gasping for breath and laughing at the unicorn, who returned the laughter.

After she had gotten her breath back, she said, "Did you do that as well? Make me dance, I mean?"

He chuckled. “Somewhat. It was a part of the healing, you see, not merely to cause it to be well, but to cause it to be used."

She laughed a little herself at that. "You must go, then? You could not stay here until they come back?"

Quickfoot shook himself all over. "No. The question you ask is important, and not merely to yourselves. I must pass along word of your coming. But I shall return this evening, for certain."

He sprang off up the slope, and was away before she could say more.

The first thing the three men noticed when they came back to the camp that evening, was that Carla was walking without the crutches. There wasn't even a trace of a limp.

"What has happened here, Carla?" asked Wissagebreht.

"A unicorn came to drink here at the pond and stopped to talk to me. While he was here, he touched my ankle with his horn and healed it."

Wissagebreht nodded, as though he had been expecting this answer. "And what did you speak of to the unicorn?"

She laughed. "Yes, I did talk about our quest, and what we had come to find out. Yssagarit said he would come back this evening and talk to all of us."

And the Wizard smiled as well. "So we have been wandering all over trying to find unicorns, and the unicorn actually came here and found you?"

She laughed again. "So it seems."

Neither Carla nor Bruderic had much appetite for supper that evening as they were too excited about Carla's meeting with the unicorn. However, Lungand was an old soldier who knew enough to eat and rest whenever there was the least opportunity. Therefore he ate and urged Bruderic to do the same. Wissagebreht nagged Carla in order to force her to eat as well. So, despite the excitement, she came close enough to eating sufficiently.

The party sat quietly waiting. Meanwhile, the two younger people fidgeted around. They continually got up, walked around, looked up at the hillside, then flopped to the ground again. Carla would occasionally put a stone in her sling and throw it at a boulder far across the stream. Sometimes she even hit it.

Just as Carla was beginning to despair that Quickfoot was not coming back, they heard the sounds of hoofbeats on the path. Then Quickfoot came trotting over the hill with two other unicorns accompanying him.

Instead of coming to talk to Wissagebreht or to Lungand, Carla was surprised that the unicorns trotted directly to where she sat and bowed their heads to her. "A good evening to you, little maiden."

"And a good evening to you as well, Yssagarit. You have returned, as you promised," Carla replied.

The unicorn laughed. "Did you doubt it? Of course we have returned. And my two companions here are Kissadwar Silverhorn, and Pharassit Shywalker. And you had a question to ask us, did you not?"

Carla shifted her attention from the unicorns slightly to note what her companions were doing. Wissagebreht sat back, relaxed, as though all this were something he had planned. Bruderic leaned forward eagerly. He appeared to be excited at seeing the elusive unicorns. Also, perhaps he was a little fearful of the answer to the question that Carla would ask. Lungand sat like a thundercloud, silent, black, and threatening. She could practically hear him thinking, 'Why do they talk to the girl? And why all this politeness and talking of nothing? Let us get the question answered!'

But he said nothing.

She gathered herself up. "It is said that the health of our land is tied to the return of the unicorns. For five years the unicorns have not returned to our land, and for five years the land has been progressively wasting away. We have come to ask why you do not return?"

Quickfoot nodded his head a trifle. "We have expected you for some time. Not necessarily this specific group of people. But we knew that at some time people would come to find out why we do not return. The answer, unfortunately lies not with us but with the Elves.

"Many years back, a young woman of the Elves met with a Prince of Men who was wandering in the woods. They talked, they fell in love, and eventually they married. The marriage came about despite misgivings from both families. Seeing that the two were determined. Both families let them have their way and give them their blessing.

"The Elves, being large-handed in these matters, promised health and prosperity for their land. And, as a sign of this, said that all would be well with the land so long as the unicorns continued to return. And so it was, for many years.

"Then the King died in an accident, and the land was troubled by its own people. Many battles were fought, and the queen was taken under the protection of one particular man. Kept alone, it is said. Except for one maid whom she had brought from among her own people, and two loyal men-at-arms.

"The man protecting the queen said that he was ruling on her behalf until the birth of her child. The war was fierce, for there were many who felt they had a better right than he to claim such rule. One by one he beat and defeated them, until he at last was left as the strongest in the realm. And during this time it began to be rumoured that he had murdered the Queen, the maid, and the two men-at-arms.

"He denied this for some time, but neither would he permit them to show themselves publicly. 'It was not safe,' he said.

"Then suddenly he announced that they had died. That the queen had died because while she was ill with the plague, her babe was born. The babe was born dead, and the Queen, worn with illness and grief, died as well. The others, the maid and the men-at-arms, had caught the plague as well from staying with her so loyally. All the bodies were burned and buried immediately to prevent the spread of the plague.

"As a result of all this, he claimed for himself the crown. Those who might have objected were already largely defeated in the wars. So the land knew peace for some time."

"The Elves do not often rush to hasty decisions. They tried for many years to discover the truth of the matter. We have no idea what answers they found, but eventually, a few years ago, they asked us to cease going to your country. That is all we know."

"So what do we do now?" burst out Lungand angrily. "We have come all this way to talk to unicorns. Now we find that it is the Elves we have to deal with, that the Elves have cursed our land."

Wissagebreht spoke more mildly. "I think it would be best not to take too negative a view of the situation, Lungand. We ought not to give up and go home simply because problem is with the Elves instead of with the unicorns."

"You think not? What else can we do? March to the Kingdom of the Elves, show ourselves there in the form of beggars, and attempt to change their minds?"

"That is not exactly what I had in mind, but near enough."

But now Lungand had gone off on another track. "You knew about the unicorns! You knew that the difficulty was with the Elves, and yet you led us off on this fruitless quest!"

As the Chamberlain paused for breath, Wissagebreht interrupted. "Supposing I had told you at the beginning that unicorns were not returning because the Elves had asked them not to. What would have your reaction been? You would have wanted to set forth immediately, gather your army, and declare war on the Elves.
"Whether or not you could have successfully fought against them is one thing. But it is almost certain that nothing you could do would force them to remove the curse."

"So as it is we go there now, humiliate ourselves, and beg them to have mercy on us?" spat Lungand as he flung his arms out in frustration.

"It is probably not necessary to humiliate ourselves. What we will have to do is explain what has happened, tell them our side of the story. Tell all the truth, and I think they will be generous."

"'All the truth?'" Lungand exploded again. "Who knows all the truth any longer? I certainly do not. I know only the story as it came to me. That my brother took the Queen and her retinue under his protection. That later on it was told that she had died, and he took the crown for want of a better-qualified claimant."

"And you never sought to discover anything more than that?", queried Wissagebreht.

"No. Perhaps I feared what I might find. Knowing that if it was as I feared, we would face another civil war. A war which the land could hardly bear", Lungand spoke lowly, yet with uncharacteristic emotion underlying his tone.

Wissagebreht merely looked at him.

After a moment Lungand spoke again, as though defending himself against accusation, "You know what manner of man my brother was, Wissagebreht. Proud and unyielding, disdainful of accusations not backed up with deeds. While he lived, all the investigation I could do was limited to those things which would not tell one of his foes that I was plotting against him. If any of them had thought that the brothers had fallen out, the war would begin again.

"And to be sure, with what I found out I could do little. I cannot prove that he had them killed or, that he did not. Had I told him I doubted his public story, he would merely have stared at me and suggested that if I doubted his word. He would have to challenge me, his brother.

"I did talk to the midwife. She agreed that the Queen was ill when the babe arrived. That the babe was female, a weak little thing with scarce strength to cry aloud. She concurs that the others present, the men-at-arms and the maid all showed signs of the plague. The seneschal had hustled her out before she could do more than bathe the babe, and she doubts that it lived out the night."

Lungand looked down at the ground for a long moment, then looked up again. "I fear that my brother had it already in his mind to claim the crown. The only witnesses at the birth were the midwife and the Queen's own people. For such a birth as this, it is normal that there be several witnesses, in order to prove that the heir is rightfully born. All we know is that the queen died giving birth to a child, an unhealthy girl child, who has never been heard of again. As to the deaths of the others. Well, during the plague-time bodies were commonly burnt, and there might well be no graves left to inspect. What more truth can we tell?"

Bruderic stood up. There were tears in his eyes, and his face was twisted with anger, "And so my father was a usurper and very likely a murderer? My claim to the throne lies only in the strength of my father's sword-arm? I will renounce all that and go to live in the wilds; perhaps that will mollify the Elves!"

Lungand would have spoken, but Wissagebreht was quicker, "Bruderic, your father may not have acted wisely in all things. Indeed, he may well have done things which were evil. You are not your father. You are yourself. There will be those who will compare you to him. Say that you show all his faults, but you must learn to ignore those and do what is right for you.

"As for renouncing the throne, that might perhaps help the situation if there were another claimant to the throne who would be acceptable to all. As it is, all you would accomplish by this is what your uncle fears. A civil war as all those who feel themselves fit to be king gather their forces against all the others."

"So I hold to what my father took illegally?" Bruderic thrust his hands out emphatically.

"For want of a better alternative, yes," Wissagebreht nodded.

He walked a few paces away, and stopped, staring at the sky which was still purple with the setting sun. Finally he turned back, "All right. I suppose my choices are to hold onto something I feel I have no right to, or to let it go and see destruction wrought. Bitter choices, but choices I must make. Tell me, Lungand, is this what it means to grow up?"

Lungand was silent for a little while, then he said, "I fear so. I would have shielded you from most of this for a little longer, had I been able. Time and chance brought it forth before I wished."

Bruderic smiled a bitter little smile, "I had heard most of it, in bits and pieces, for many years. Embroidered and embellished or trimmed and minimized, depending on the speaker. Yet at the time you told me very little, avoiding any direct questions, so that I could pretend the worst of it was not so. But I think I always knew that there was more to it than mere jealousy."

He was quiet for a while, then he brought his shoulders back and looked at Wissagebreht and Lungand, "So, then. When do we go to visit the Elves?"

Lungand looked at Wissagebreht, "You obviously wish to go from here, without returning to the kingdom."

Wissagebreht nodded, "Should we return, only for a moment, I fear it might lead to entanglements we do not wish. Such as some Lords desiring to send out an army with us, and I think our purpose can be achieved by this small company. As to when we leave, tomorrow will be soon enough for that."

"Tomorrow, then," said Bruderic.

"But one other thing," said Wissagebreht, turning his attention to the unicorns, "Will you accompany us?"

Quickfoot tossed his head. "Certainly. We can even carry you, if you will agree to certain limitations."

"What would those be?"

"We will not be bridled or tied. We will go as quickly as we go, without urging from you. And we will stop when and as we feel it necessary. But I can assure you that we will travel farther and faster in a day than you could afoot."

Wissagebreht nodded. "So be it. For my part, I will agree, and I think the others will also agree."

Carla, thinking of the long trek from Wissagebreht's hut, agreed readily. Bruderic was no less willing. Lungand, deep in thought, had to be questioned again. But, when they got his attention, he said absently, "What? Oh, yes, of course."

"Good, then," said the wizard. "Best that we rest for the night, then, and be ready to start early in the morning."

In the morning, the unicorns were there before the four were finished breakfast. But the unicorns waited politely until they were packed and ready to leave. Carla got on Quickfoot, with Bruderic behind her. Wissagebreht and the Chamberlain mounted the other two.

"Ready?" asked Quickfoot.

"Yes," they answered.

"Then let us be away." And the three unicorns set off at a quick trot.

For the first little while, Carla tried to find a comfortable way to sit on the unicorn's back. Quickfoot's spine was very hard, and jouncing along as he galloped was a bruising experience. Eventually, she hit upon a method which involved moving as the unicorn moved. A method which was a little less painful. She was then able to pay attention to the trip. She noticed, with some satisfaction, that they were moving farther and faster than they could hope to move by foot.

She could also think about where they were going. To the Kingdom of the Elves! She knew stories about the Elves. She knew that the Dark Elves were enemies of men, cruel and vindictive. Where the Light Elves had little at all to do with men, though trust between men and Elves had never been high.

From what Carla knew through the stories, it was possible that the Elves would simply ignore the party and allow them to wander through the Elven Kingdom. However, they would never come into contact with anyone who would help them on their quest. In that matter Carla was quite certain that Wissagebreht likely had some scheme in mind which would bring them to the notice of the Elves.

The unicorns, seemingly tireless, trotted on and on. it was Wissagebreht who finally called them to a halt. "We all need a rest, and perhaps some of us could do with a drink of water. Let us stop for a moment, Quickfoot."

They stopped. All the people got down, stretched, and walked around a little. They then drank a little water. By the time that Carla was beginning to notice how sore and stiff her legs were, Wissagebreht had them mounted up and riding again.

They stopped again several times during the day. While at night, Carla was almost certain that her legs would never be the same again. Lungand spent much of that evening in a dark mood. Bruderic whispered to Carla, "Be careful around him now. He is worrying about what might be happening in the kingdom with both of us away."

She nodded. As she walked around the campfire, though, she noticed from time to time that Lungand was looking at her with a strange expression on his face. She went to Wissagebreht and told him. He smiled and nodded.

"Don't worry. Something has suddenly occurred to him, and that has many ramifications. I see it too, and I will do my best to see that no harm comes to you from it."

"Harm? Harm from what? noticed, then?" What is it that he has noticed, then?"

“If I tell you that, then the two of you would be goose-stepping around each other until something inevitably went wrong. Do you remember that I promised to tell you about your heritage once this was all over? Well, this is a part of it and I will explain it to you later. Now go, talk to the unicorns and stop worrying.”

She went to talk to the unicorns, but she was unable to stop worrying. Who could she be that Lungand would be so concerned about? She was only a girl. About sixteen years old, and about the time of the queen's disappearance she would barely have been born.

It struck her then, almost like a blow. Lungand thought that she might be the child of the Queen! The midwife had said that the babe had been a girl, and very feeble. What if the babe had not died, but had been kept alive. Had been secretly taken out of the place where they had all been kept. Perhaps by one of the loyal men-at-arms, and delivered to the hut of Wissagebreht as one person who might keep her safe?

She shook her head. No, if that were true, Wissagebreht would have said or done something before now. She had dreamed of her real parents coming and taking back to their great castle, but those were only dreams. She could not believe that she was a Queen. Of course, that need not mean a thing to Lungand. All he saw was a girl who was about the right age to be the rightful heir to the throne. Possibly, to be the cause of that same civil war he feared so much.

But who was she? Well, all she could do was to wait until all this business was over, and the Wizard would tell her.

Another day passed similarly to the first, the only thing that changed was the landscape, as there were soft rolling hills, and every so often an outcropping of trees. On the morning of the third day Carla found that the stiffness due to the unaccustomed riding was passing. However, it appeared to be giving way to soreness and chafing due to the constant rubbing in the saddle. It grew so bad that she thought that she'd never be free of it.

Wissagebreht pawed through his bag until he found something, a small pot, and he gave it to her. "Here, rub this where your legs are sorest. It will help for a while, and I hope that a while is all that will be needed."

By the middle of the day they were in a country of gently rolling hills. As the unicorns reached the tops of some of the higher hills, they could make out a faint dark green line far away on the horizon. They made their camp on one of those hills. After they had dismounted, Wissagebreht looked off in that direction and said, "There they are. The woods where the Elves dwell."

The next day took them even closer to the woods, and the day after that they were at its edge. The trees of the Lothbosc had been large and old, but within this forest there were larger and older trees. Great oaks twisted their limbs as they reached across the path to each other and intertwined. In between them sycamores sprouted up here and there, like children trying to get their parent's attention. There was a feeling about it. Not the kind of dread and hate in the Lothbosc. But something more subtle. A hint that strangers might come in if they behaved themselves. But they were not really wanted, and the woods would ignore them.

Lungand looked around, and his thoughts were plain. Whatever he had expected, it was not this! "What now, Wizard? Do we walk about shouting, and hope to be brought to their notice?"

The Wizard merely smiled a mild smile and said, "Not quite. Let us go a little further in before we worry too much over that."

They went further in among the great trunks of the trees. Along a path which seemed sometimes to be hardly there at all. Quickfoot snorted suddenly, "The Elves are here. They are watching us and listening. They will wait with great patience to see if they can find out what it is we want in their lands. But they may never come forth."

Lungand looked at the unicorn, "How can you tell?"

Quickfoot laughed, "Perhaps what is hidden from the eyes of men is not hidden from the eyes of unicorns. Or perhaps indeed you do not wish to see or hear what is around you."

"They are there," said Wissagebreht, "I cannot see or hear them, but I know that they are here. So we must bring them out to talk to us."

"And how are we to do that? Shout at them? Call insults down on their families?" Lungand sneered.

"Lungand, for a man who has kept a kingdom full of potentially rebellious subjects at peace for the past ten years, you show remarkably little patience. Let us camp here the night, and if they have not come out to talk to us by morning, then I will do something."

They set up their camp, all the while with a growing feeling that they were being watched. They sang no songs around that night's campfire, but rather told quiet tales of bygone days.

As the evening wore on, Carla noticed that Bruderic was becoming more and more morose. She had taken to sitting as away from him as possible, but now she began to feel a little sorry for him. Neither of the two men seemed to be taking any notice of his mood, so she decided that something should be done. She moved around closer to him, "We are almost at the end of our quest, Bruderic. Should you not be happy?"

"Happy?", He gave her a painful grimace. "I am a King because my father stole the kingdom, probably murdering the Queen and her child in the process. And because of that, throughout my days there will be men who feel that they have as good a claim to the throne as I. So from time to time I must fight, not the enemies of my people, but my own people. Perhaps the Elves will demand of me that I renounce the throne. That would please me greatly."

"No," said Carla, "I doubt that they would ask something of you that would be so easily accomplished. But I think you are partly right. It is you of whom they will ask something, for it is you that represent the Kingdom."

He sighed. "Yes, it is, is it not? Just as my uncle has always pointed out to me, there will be consequences to anything I do with the Kingdom. And my choice must always be to do that which will cause the least harm in the long run.

Carla shuddered. "And I thought I had a hard life. Living in a tumbledown hut with an old wizard, trying to patch up the cracks when the wind blew through."

He smiled a little. "Yes, there is that. I live warmly most of the time. Though when I visit the castles of some of my barons, as I must do out of courtesy from time to time. I discover that they were built for defence, not for comfort. Why I remember a time..."

And he went on to tell a humorous story about one such visit. A long story, tedious at times, but with a funny little twist at the end. Carla was pleased to see the gloom lift from his face a little as he went on.

When morning came, the Elves still had not come out to speak to them. Lungand was clearly angry at the whole thing. So much so that it was not likely that he could contribute anything useful to any discussion of the subject. Bruderic, however, was concerned. At least he was concerned about getting this over and done with. "Well, wizard, what do we do now?"

Wissagebreht smiled. "Why we draw them out. Come, Carla, there is a song I want you to sing. Here, follow this:

'The stars shone bright in the summer night

As the Princess danced in the wood.

And a man who came from death and flame

Beneath the great trees stood.

O' the flowers were fair which decked her hair

And light were her feet on the ground.

So fair she seemed that he felt he dreamed

And he dared not make a sound.'"

There was much more to the song, which told the long story of Dagobreht, the King and Guendatha, Princess of the Elves. The song told how they met. How he loved her. How he wooed her and won her despite the objections of her people. How he finally won his throne, and took her to share it with him.

By the time she as well into the song, Carla felt that someone was paying close attention to the party. As it ended, there was a movement in the brush and suddenly ten Elves were standing all around them. The Elves had bows with arrows held loosely on the strings. Save for one, the apparent leader, who carried bow in his right hand at his side and looked at them with an expression of disdain on his face.

They were all slender of build, but even so, they carried themselves as warriors who knew their own abilities well. They all seemed young, with fair hair and blue or blue-green eyes. Each wore a hooded shirt of mottled green and brown over a chain-mail hauberk. Their trousers and shoes, again were of mottled green and brown.

The leader continued to survey the four. At last, after Carla had begun to feel quite uncomfortable, he spoke. "Who are you, and how is it that you have the audacity to sing that song in this place?"

Bruderic and Lungand had put hands to their sword-hilts. But Wissagebreht made a motion with his hand to tell them not to worry. He himself smiled at the Elves and spoke quietly. "I am Wissagebreht, a Wizard, and I may be known to many of your people if not to yourself. The girl is my ward, Carla. These others are Bruderic, King of Vorholm and his Uncle and Chamberlain, Lungand."

The face was set and grim, the eyes burned with anger, “and if you are a wise wizard, known to the Elves, what brought you to sing the song of Guendatha in the very home of the Elves?"

Wissagebreht shrugged. "It pleased the Elves to hide about our camp and spy on us, waiting to hear who we were and what we wanted. There is, however, a little urgency about our quest. Therefore, knowing that it would get your attention, I had my ward sing the song."

Carla, listening to the conversation and watching the Elves, felt more than a little fear that Wissagebreht was going too far. That the leader of the Elves was near to ordering his archers to make pincushions out of the four. She felt glad that about that moment Quickfoot moved over beside her. She leaned an arm on his withers. A moment later the Elf, surveying the group, relaxed a little. It seemed that it was the presence of the unicorns as much as anything which brought about this relaxation.

"So, then. What is this quest, and what is its urgency?"

Wissagebreht shook his head. "Shall we be required to speak of our quest to every Elf who wanders by? We wish to speak to the King."

Carla, amazed at his boldness in the circumstances, leaned a little harder on the unicorn. Quickfoot turned his head back and looked at her with those blue eyes. She calmed herself.

"In this case, you shall have to speak of your quest to me at least. I am Mabbren, son of the Elf King, and I do know you, at least by reputation, Wissagebreht. But the days have gone by when there was close friendship between Men and Elves. In recent years, there have been more reasons for Elves to fear and dislike Men. Including the end of Guendatha, which is not spoken of in the song so prettily sung by your ward."

He bowed slightly towards Carla, and there was a feeling of lessening tension. He made some kind of quick sign with his hand, and his warriors relaxed. Letting their bows drop to their sides, though none of them changed their expressions. If Mabbren was allowing himself to be convinced of the friendliness of the group, it did not seem to be passed on to his followers.

He continued. "In addition to being the son of the Elf King, I am also the guardian of this part of the wood. It is my responsibility to watch and question wanderers and vagabonds in these woods. So, I must insist that you tell me of your quest. If it is sufficiently important, I can assure you that you will be sent on immediately to the King."

Wissagebreht looked at the Elf for a moment, then nodded. "So be it, then. This is our quest."

And he went on to describe briefly the reasons why they had come, first to find the unicorns, then to visit the Elves. Mabbren listened with patience. Frowning a little as the Wizard described Yssagarit's story of the disappearance of the Queen.

When the tale was done, Mabbren stood silent for a moment, and spoke at last. "So, there were those among us who had expected that at some time or another Men would come to ask us to remove the curse. My father himself has occasionally wondered when you would come."

"And here we are. Will you then take us to the King your father?"

Mabbren nodded. "Oh, yes, I shall take you, though you may have little joy of the meeting. My father has from time to time expressed his distrust of Men and his displeasure at all their works. And remember that Guendatha was his sister's daughter."

Wissagebreht shrugged. "Yes, I know all this. Yet it is necessary to try to convince him."

"Then I will take you to him," said Mabbren.

He chose two of his followers to accompany them. he then assigned one other to take charge in his absence, and they prepared to march.

Chapter 5

THE ELVES

Mabbren led them on a seemingly invisible path through grass and shrubs. They met once with a party of Elves headed the other way, these were not warriors like Mabbren, however, they did carry swords at their sides. They were mounted on horses, large white beasts, whom they rode without benefit of bit or bridle. The horses seemed to know where to go without being told, stepping carefully through the sunlit forest.

The Elves who rode the horses were all dressed in fine brightly coloured silks, and they sang in Elven as they came. Even though she couldn't understand the words, Carla almost felt she knew what they were singing about.

It was a song of joy and sadness. Of trees growing from tiny saplings. Growing up, suffering through windstorms and hard winters. Falling under the woodsman's axe. Growing until at last they could grow no more. Then ceasing to come into leaf and falling silently into decay. But at the end the song leaped up into joy again, for at the foot of the dead tree was another small sapling growing.

The singers were a fair people, more beautiful than anything Carla had ever seen. They smiled at Mabbren and hailed him in their own language. As he returned the greeting and explained his errand. Carla saw the eyes of the Elves turn to the four of them, and felt a feeling of anger and sadness coming from them. Silently they moved around Mabbren's group and silently rode on down the trail. But just before they passed out of sight, Carla heard another song starting.

They continued on the path which wound its way through the forest. Eventually, they came around a curve in the trail and suddenly before them was a city. A city of spires and towers of gold and silver. Walls studded with precious stones and carven ornamentation. From the towers heraldic devices flew. The front gates were huge oak planks bound with brass bands. The brass carved with various scenes of life and adventure. Mabbren came to the gate and pulled a cord which dangled down from one side of the gateway.

A small concealed window in the gate opened, and a face appeared. Mabbren spoke quietly in his own language, then the great gate began to creak open. He turned to the others. "Enter then, Drefcwed of the woods, the city of the King, Urddas."

They entered the city and it was just as magnificent on the inside of the walls as it had been on the outside. Carla marvelled at the sights, sounds and smells within. Elves wandered about in brightly coloured, whimsical costumes. There was the sound of singing floating down on a breeze while unfamiliar instruments played off at a distance. Carla took in a deep breath and was greeted by the comforting smell of pastries baking. Just inside the gate, they were led to a small stone building which looked like a prison.

"You must wait here until the King summons you," stated Mabbren.

"We wait in prison, then?" Wissagebreht's brows lowered.

"You must wait somewhere until the King is informed of your presence," repeated Mabbren.

"In prison?" bristled Wissagebreht.

Mabbren frowned and put a hand to his sword. After a moment he relaxed. "So, then. If it pleases you to wait around in the King's porch until he calls for you, do so."

Wissagebreht relaxed also. They followed Mabbren along the winding street, while Carla tried hard to see and hear everything that was to be seen and heard. All she retained though, was a confused impression of bright colours, music, and strange smells.

They arrived at last at the palace of the King. It was a stately building. The door of which consisted of a stone step mounted between two tall trees, and a large wooden doorway fixed in to the trunks. The doorway was open and two Elves stood guard, leaning on long spears, watching the road. Mabbren hailed them in his own language, and they spoke back and forth for a bit. The guards eventually giving the four a darkly suspicious look.

"Go inside," said Mabbren. "There is a bench in there on which you can sit until the King agrees to see you. The animals will have to stay outside."

Wissagebreht nodded shortly, and they tied the pony to a low branch on one of the gate trees. Quickfoot said, "We will wait here too. This is the way the Elves are, dark and secret, too careful of strangers, but at last open and generous. Don't worry."

"I hope you're right," Carla said, "but right now things don't look very hopeful. They're treating us as though we were criminals."

They went inside and found the bench where they sat and waited. At first that was not too difficult, but after some minutes with no word, Carla and Bruderic both began to fidget. Lungand was seated quietly staring at the wall opposite him, anger plain in his face. While Wissagebreht sat with his eyes shut and a placid countenance.

For a little while it was possible to sit on the bench and wait. Then they began shuffling their feet around and staring at the careful workmanship in the tapestries on the walls. But eventually, Carla and Bruderic both found that they had to do more than that. The first few times that they got up from their seats, Lungand called them back with a quiet but definitely warning voice. At the fourth time he opened his mouth to speak, then closed it again and tried to ignore them.

Finally, they were sent for. A very young Elf came to inform them that the King would see them now, and that he would show them the way. They walked down fair hallways, delicate friezework had been elegantly crafted into the crown of the molding and each hallway was more handsomely decorated than the last. They continued on until at last they came to the throne room.

The throne room was a wide-open area. It was well-lit, with a great space between the door and the two thrones set up at the back. On the right-hand throne sat an Elf, erect and kingly, with a crown of gold on his head. He was dressed in white, he had a long but neatly-trimmed beard. Across his knees lay a sceptre, a white rod as long as his arm. It seemed at first that the rod was made of stone. But as they came closer, Carla could see that it was actually some kind of finely polished wood.

He himself looked very stern and forbidding from a distance. But again as they drew closer, Carla saw in his face something which she could only describe as being like Wissagebreht. A stern old man, but one who could still laugh and joke when the circumstances were right. But at present he was going to demand justice. There was a shudder in Carla's mind at what such a stern person would demand as justice.

On the left-hand throne was a lady, and she was also dressed all in white. Like the King, she was fair to look on, though she bore no sceptre. She, too, looked stern and forbidding, but there seemed very much more of natural kindness in her face. As she looked on the four, worn and weary from their travels, the look on her face became one of concern.

The young Elf led them to what was considered a proper distance from the thrones.

Then he drew himself up and announced, "Milord King Urddas, Milady Queen Serenglas, I present to you these four from the Kingdom of Vorholm come to beg a favour."

The King's eyes fell on them. "What favour would you have from me?"

There was a short pause. Wissagebreht shot a look at Bruderic, who was waiting for Lungand to speak for him, as he had been used to do. Indeed, the Chamberlain was about to speak when Bruderic realized that, as King, it was his right to speak for the Kingdom. "Milord King, I am Bruderic, King of Vorholm. I understand that you have put our land under a curse, holding the unicorns from their usual return in order to signify this to us. I have come to ask you to lift this curse."

The King of the Elves looked at the King of Vorholm. His expression was stern, but there was no condemnation in it. "On that score, there are several problems. I am sure that you are aware that my niece, Guendatha, was wed to the King of Vorholm. Can you tell me what was her fate?"

Bruderic lifted his chin. "As near as I can tell, she died. There was a time of trouble in the Kingdom, a time in which my father played a part. As a babe at the time, I have no first-hand knowledge, nor have I heard more than rumour and innuendo. My father was keeping the Queen and her small retinue, ruling, he said, in her name. The story was told that she died in the night when she gave birth to her own child. But there appear to have been no witnesses to say whether there was or was not foul play. There are other tales, depending on whether the teller loved or hated my father, but that is all I can say."

While Bruderic spoke, the King of the Elves watched his face. When he had done, Urddas nodded, slowly. "So it seems. We have tried to find the truth of all this, but truth seems hard to come by. We had hoped that someone would come from your court to explain the manner of our niece's death, and no one came. At last, seeking to draw some response, we withdrew our blessing from your land. By asking the unicorns to cease going there as a sign of that. And hoping that someone there, such as Wissagebreht, would know what it meant."

He looked at the Wizard briefly, then continued.

"So now you have come at last, but you can add little or nothing to what we already know. And the matter remains unresolved. Was our niece murdered, or did she merely die in childbirth? And in the latter case, how much was her death a result of considered neglect? We cannot know. Only our little knowledge of the personalities involved makes us suspicious. What do you say, King of Vorholm?"

Bruderic was quiet for a moment, then he spoke. "My people suffer. From the greatest lords In their castles to the peasants in their huts, they suffer. Many of them know little or nothing of the fate of Queen Guendatha; why should they be punished?"

"And why should the death of our niece go unpunished?", King Urddas questioned slowly as though to contain his anger.

Bruderic drew a deep breath. "So be it. If punishment there must be, let it fall on me alone, not on my people. For indeed, I alone can be shown to have profited from the death of your niece."

Lungand drew a deep breath and seemed about to speak, but Bruderic gave him a warning look, and he subsided. There was wrath on his brow, however.

The Elf-King sat silent for a time. He was thinking deeply about all that had been said. It was clear from what little expression was on his face that what had been said found little favour with him.

At last he spoke, and there was deep feeling in his voice. "She is dead, then, and none knows where her body was laid?"

"Lord," answered Bruderic, "She was ill with the plague when she died, and the custom at the time was to burn the bodies of those who died of plague."

"Dead and burned to ashes," said the Elf-king in a terrible voice, "with nothing to say that she ever lived, save the memories of those who loved her!"

He stood and stepped down from his throne, and went back through a curtain behind it, his head downcast.

The four stood, wondering what to do next, but before they could do anything, the Queen spoke. "You have brought distressing news, travellers. I regret that my husband must leave so hastily, but you must understand." She turned to address the young Elf who had shown them into the presence of the King. "Go quickly, bring seats for these four, and have something brought for them to drink."

As the Elf went quickly out on these errands, the Queen spoke again. "You came here accompanied by three unicorns. How did you come by them?"

Wissagebreht bowed. "Mostly my doing, Milady Queen. I knew that if I informed them that they must come here to the Elven Kingdom. They would not come in any proper frame of mind, might even attempt to bring arms and soldiers here. I misled them a little by telling them that we must first find the unicorns. and that to do so would require a very small party. So we went to find the unicorns first."

"And how did you do that? The nature of the unicorns is well-known, that they are shy and retiring, not coming readily to Men."

Wissagebreht smiled. "My ward," he indicated Carla, "was lame, and had to stay by our campsite while we three went searching. The unicorn found her, and thus the first part of our quest was fulfilled."

"Really?" The Queen turned her gaze fully on Carla now, and her eyes widened slightly. "Come here, child."

Carla hesitated, and the Queen smiled. "Come, child, I will not harm you."

Carla approached the Queen. As she drew near, she became more and more conscious of the state of her clothing. Moreover, the fact that she had been travelling for a long while without having had the chance to wash. The Queen extended a hand, and Carla extended hers. Letting Serenglas take her tanned and roughened hand in her own white one. "Who are your parents, child?"

"I-I d-don't know," stuttered Carla, then, gaining confidence, "I was left with Wissagebreht as a babe, and that is all I know, Milady Queen."

The Queen looked beyond her to the Wizard, "Wissagebreht, do you know who your ward is?"

"Yes, Milady Queen, I know.", He answered.

She laughed, "Come, then! Must I draw the secret from you, word by word? Who is she? She is of partly Elven blood, that much I can tell, but who is she?"

"Milady Queen, the tale of the love of Dagobreht and Guendatha is a popular tale. But none know of the other love between Elf and Man that came about at the same time. When Guendatha came to live with Dagobreht, she brought with her a maid. Another Elf-woman, named Calongwir. One of the men-at-arms set by Dagobreht to be bodyguard for the Queen was Driwhelm. The two were cast much into each other's company, and came to love each other deeply.
"Yet ere they could make their love known openly, or seek permission to wed, the King died. All was thrown into turmoil. Among the various lords who sought the crown, the only one to say that he fought on behalf of the Queen. Who was the very same one who was keeping them imprisoned. though the imprisonment might be very comfortable.

"Thus they came together for whatever comfort they might find in each other's arms. Calongwir came to be with child, a fact which was never revealed to anyone. As is the way of such things, her child came some time before the queen's child. This brought to the two a new concern. For where they had once to be concerned only for their own safety, they now had a child as well.

"They arranged that Driwhelm should take the child out to safety. There was no question of the Queen escaping in her condition. The exertions to which Driwhelm himself was put would have been impossible.

"When he had gotten free of the castle, Driwhelm knew that he could not leave the babe with anyone in the immediate area. He felt that the safest place would be with me, for I had never made a secret of my distress over the situation of the Queen and her imprisonment.

"He brought her to me, told me the story, and went back to try to free Calongwir. I do not know what happened after that; I only know that he never returned, nor was he spoken of again. I then raised the child, and never spoke of her origin, for fear that someone might consider her an inconvenient reminder of the past."

"You could have brought her here.", Said the Queen.

Wissagebreht shrugged. "And then what? There were already Elves who felt that Guendatha was ill treated. And this story would only have made more trouble for the Kingdom. And as well, how would she have been accepted among you? A child of mixed blood, mixed with the same blood that had treated your own so cruelly?

"Nor had I intended to hold her heritage from her forever. In a year or two from now, at the most, I had intended to bring her here to show to you, to see what would be your sentiment. By that time, of course, she would be better able to understand, and if you rejected her, she could better endure it."

The Queen nodded her understanding of all this. Carla stood there, stunned. not knowing what to make of all this. So she did have parents, and one of those parents had been an Elf-woman, the maid to the Queen Guendatha! Did she have other family living, then, among the Elves? Or, as Wissagebreht had hinted, might they not want to know about her? Or perhaps indeed they might invite her to visit them to stay with them.

"Still, you might have tried. What's done is done, though. Ah, here are the chairs and the refreshment! Sit down, Carla. We may have to talk more about this."

Carla was so surprised by the news that she barely tasted the drink. It was some sort of beverage of mixed fruit and berry juices, and quite refreshing. There were also some sort of little cakes, baked with honey and a number of spices. Which were very welcome after all the travelling and excitement.

The curtain behind the thrones opened, and the King came out as suddenly as he had gone. His face was like a face carved in stone, with no anger in it, merely determination. He saw the four seated, drinking, and glanced quickly at the Queen. He then looked back at the four.

Before he could speak, Serenglas said, "Milord King, the girl, Carla, is the daughter of Calongwir."

The King looked at Carla, and she felt a twinge of fear. "Calongwir? She was not wed!"

"No, Milord, but Wissagebreht has told me the story of how the child came to be born. And there is no denying that she has Elvish blood in her.", The Queen said calmly.

The King looked at her again. "No, there is not. And had I not been so concerned with other things, I would have seen it myself. But we must deal with that later; there is the question of Vorholm to be dealt with."

Everyone sat up straight.

The King sighed. "King Bruderic, you have suggested that any punishment should be yours to bear. I do not agree."

Bruderic was about to start to his feet when the King held up a hand. "Let me finish. No punishment could bring back Guendatha; she is dead and gone. But there must be an atonement."

"Atonement? I am willing to make whatever atonement is in my power if it will spare my land from the trouble it is presently undergoing."

Urddas gave him an approving look.

"Spoken like a true King, Bruderic of Vorholm. Hear then my judgement. You shall go to the Dwarves and ask of them a memorial for Guendatha, which will be set up on a public monument in your kingdom as a remembrance."

"What sort of memorial did you wish?"

"That will be for the Dwarves to decide. They are skilled in all crafts, and will certainly be able to devise something fitting. Only be certain that it is you yourself who go to them. The Dwarves are also careful bargainers, and it is for you to fulfil their conditions."

Bruderic nodded. "So. If you will permit us to stay this night, we will leave in the morning."

The Elf-King nodded. "You may stay the night as our guests. But you will not see me again until the time that you have fulfilled the conditions I have set for you."

He turned to the young Elf and said, "Get them rooms, see that they have everything they need. It will not be said that the guests of the Elves are ill treated."

Once again he rose from his throne, and without a word of leave-taking, went through the curtain behind it. The Queen also rose, but she did not hurry away immediately.

"You mean well," she said, "And clearly you are willing to go into unknown danger for your people. Good fortune go with you all."

And she, too, left them.

A young Elf servant led them to a set of fair rooms set in another wing of the castle. The rooms were brightly lit. On the walls hung tapestries depicting events from the history of the Elvish people. There were also soft beds which looked almost too luxurious to sleep on. Wissagebreht followed Carla into her room to make sure she settled in alright. Bruderic and Lungand, after peering into their rooms came to Carla's, following along behind the Elf Servant.

"If you wish," the servant Elf told them, "water will be brought immediately for you to bathe in."

Wissagebreht nodded, "Very good."

The Elf bowed and went out. When he had gone, Carla and Lungand both turned on the Wizard and began to speak at once. The Chamberlain, having the loudest voice, was able to overwhelm her.

"The child is half-Elf, daughter of the maid of Guendatha?", Lungand stared intently at Wissagebreht as though to draw the answer from him merely by staring at him.

"So I told the King. I did not lie then, and I do not lie now.", Wissagebreht met his gaze evenly.

"She is not the daughter of Guendatha herself?", Lungand asked with a definite sound of uncertainty in his voice.

"No. You need not fear an heir to Dagobreht come to unseat your own nephew.", Reassured Wissagebreht.

"You are sure of this?", Lungand pressed.

"Yes," Wissagebreht was being quite patient. Carla could see though, that it might not be long until he ceased to tolerate this sort of questioning.

"How are you sure?" persisted Lungand.

"By what Driwhelm told me," Answered Wissagebreht.

"And might he himself not have hatched this story, with or without your aid, to keep the child safe until she came of age?", sneered Lungand.

"And might not your brother's castle have come tumbling down to bury him before he even thought to seek the crown? I tell you now, Lungand, that only so far will I allow my truthfulness to be questioned. Carla is the daughter of Driwhelm and Calongwir. She was brought to me for safety, as I have already said. And I have raised her as I did in order to keep her safe from those who might consider her a reminder of things best forgotten. And, if it comes down to it, prevent anyone noting the same coincidence of her birth and the Queen's death and using her as a figurehead for a new war. I will say no more to you on the subject." And with that, he turned his back on the Chamberlain and faced Carla. "Come, my dear, we have things to speak of."

He led Carla over to a couple of bedside chairs and sat down beside her. "I knew that by bringing you here, my dear, I risked the story of your birth coming out before I was able to prepare you. But I had to bring you along, mostly for your own sake. I told Urddas and I told Lungand all the reasons why I had to keep your origin a secret. Do you have any questions?"

Carla opened her mouth to speak. But she realized that the only things she had to ask were questions that had already been answered. She closed her mouth and thought. It was so confusing. Until just this afternoon, she had known nothing about her parents. Now she knew practically everything, and it did not seem to have changed her at all. But it should have changed her, shouldn't it?

"You knew my mother?", It was all she could think to ask.

"Yes," Wissagebreht replied.

"And my father?"

"Yes."

"What were they like?", asked Carla.

He hesitated, and she could see him casting his mind back to bring the memories to the present. "Your mother was tall and fair. She had much the look of Queen Serenglas, without so much of the regal and unapproachable air. Your father was a brave soldier, of course, for none but the bravest would be chosen to guard the Queen. He was not over tall, which perhaps accounted for much of his bravery. For he felt that he was small, and must always make up for that smallness by being the most valiant.

"And they both loved you very much." Carla began to protest but Wissagebreht raised his hand for her to pause, "Yes, I know, they sent you away to be raised by someone else. But remember their circumstances. They were in prison, be it never so comfortable a prison, and the plague was among them. Had you stayed, well, the plague commonly strikes the youngest and the weakest. And besides that, I fear that no matter what protestations were made by Lungand, his brother Hauhmot probably had no intention of giving up the throne. So they all were undoubtedly doomed, whatever happened. So they did their best for you in an impossible situation."

"Why did my father leave me with you? Why not take me directly to the Elves?", Carla still not understanding.

"That would be a long ride, and take him far from his loved one and his duty. In the meantime, Hauhmot might well decide to be done with them all, and Driwhelm would not be able even to attempt to protect the Queen. He chose me, for the reasons you already know, as being the next best thing."

There was still too much. Too many things to think about. Most of the questions she thought about asking either had already been answered, or were so petty she was ashamed to speak them at this time. Wissagebreht still sat, watching her, waiting with loving patience.

She finally spoke again. "Wissagebreht, can I wait for a while and talk to you again about all this? Right now I don't know what I want to know, what I should ask, what—" she broke off, being unable to talk further.

The Wizard nodded. "Certainly. You have had everything put on you unawares, and I apologize again. But I am ready to talk to you whenever you feel the need."

He rose and went away. She sat quietly picking at the arm of the chair, still wondering about what she had learned.

When she looked up, Bruderic was looking at her with some sort of strange expression on his face. Something that seemed akin to fright. When he saw her looking at him, he turned quickly away and began studying one of the tapestries on the walls, then quickly made his way to his own room.

She felt a sudden irrational anger at him. Then wondered why he should make her angry, for he had never tried to do anything to her except be kind. She was still wondering about this when the young Elf servant came to announce that baths were ready for them all.

Clean clothes had also been made ready for them. An Elf had come to take away the clothing they had been wearing to be washed. It took Carla some time to get used to the clothing that had been left for them. The gown was fine, much finer than anything she had ever had before. She was afraid to bump against anything or touch anything, for fear of soiling it.

The top was fitted, and flowed down into a full skirt that reached to her ankles, and moved as she walked. The sleeves were puffed, and gathered at her wrists. It was a silvery-green in colour, and fit so well that she wondered if it had been made magically for her.

The warm bath had not only washed away the dirt, it had relaxed muscles which had been tense all day. As a result, she soon began to feel extremely sleepy. When a young Elf came to announce that dinner was being set up in Wissagebreht's room, Carla could barely force herself to rise.

The short walk to the Wizard's Chamber was not enough to wake her sufficiently for anything but eating. None of the men tried to draw her into conversation. A fact which pleased her. What with her relaxation, coupled with the new knowledge of her birth spinning in her head, she was unfit to respond to anything much beyond pleasantries regarding the quality of the meal. When she thought about it later by herself, She suspected that Wissagebreht had guessed how she felt and had warned the other two.

She noticed that Bruderic stared at her strangely when first she came in. Often during the meal, she would catch his eyes on her with a strange new expression in them. It was as if he had never seen her before. She wondered about that, but she was much too tired to really give it serious thought. Very shortly after leaving the table and returning to her room, she carefully took off the gown and set it aside. Then she got into the bed, and was asleep within minutes.

She woke in the morning a little unsure of where she was. She had dreamed. Some of the dreams had been frightening. Others pleasant, but when she woke she could remember none of them.

She had debated whether to put on the green gown or her old clothes, which had been returned. She knew they would be leaving today, but she was not sure exactly when. She decided on the gown; she could change out of it quickly enough when the time came. She wondered, idly, if she could take it with her, then called herself a fool. "What would you do with such a thing, living in a wizard's hut?"

The Elves had taken the trouble to leave a large bowl of fruit in each room. As such, when breakfast was announced Carla was nibbling on a tasty peach.

The men were in their trail clothes. After a moment, she decided not to let herself be concerned about that, but rather to enjoy the feel of the gown.

They had just finished their breakfast when the young Elf came in once more. "Her Majesty Queen Serenglas is coming. She would have a few words with you before you leave."

Wissagebreht nodded. "I thought perhaps she might."

A moment later, the door opened and the Queen stepped in. The four came to their feet. She smiled at them. "Sit, sit! You will have enough and to spare of being on your feet before too long. I came to speak to Carla, first of all. Carla, as a daughter of our people you need not leave; you will be welcomed here."

Carla had never expected this. She looked to Wissagebreht, but he only smiled. "No, Carla, I will not make this decision for you. You must decide for yourself."

She looked at Bruderic, but he was too startled to say anything. He had a look on his face, something akin to fear, and that made Carla angry. Why should he be afraid? It was she that was having to deal with so many new things!

The Queen was still waiting patiently for Carla to answer. Carla pulled her thoughts together. She could stay here in this lovely place. Perhaps find a family, people who would love her, and she need not live in a drafty shack any longer. But she looked at Wissagebreht, who for years had been the only father she had known. Surely, her unknown family could never learn to love her as much as he did. He and the others were about to go off on another trip, a dangerous journey. No, she could not desert them now.

"Your majesty, I would very much like to accept your invitation. But I have started on a quest with these others, and I must finish it."

She wanted to say more, to try to ask if it would be acceptable for her to come another time, but the words refused to come.

"I thought as much. Your faith to your companions does you credit. And it does them credit as well; I hope that they all appreciate it. But you will not be on this quest forever. When it is done, come back to us. There will always be a welcome here for you."

Carla could barely stammer her thanks. The Queen put her at ease with a smile and said, "My husband cannot bring himself to wish you a safe journey. Though I know that he wishes you no ill. For myself, I wish you a safe journey on your quest, and success in the end. Go with starlight on your feet."

She turned and was gone.

Carla looked at her companions. She saw that Bruderic's expression had changed to one of relief, and she wondered what he was thinking of. Perhaps he had been frightened by the presence of Queen Serenglas, and was relieved that she had left them.

Wissagebreht looked around at the little group. "Well, best we should be on our way as soon as possible. Shall we make ready?"

He looked at Carla, and she nodded. "I will be dressed in a moment."

She hurried back to her room and changed out of the green gown into her old worn brown dress. She looked at the gown, considered folding it carefully and putting it in her pack. Eventually, she decided regretfully that it really wasn't hers. It had only been borrowed, and she could not take it. But she could come back some day! She left the gown carefully laid out full length on the bed, and went to join the men.

Bruderic was still giving her strange looks. But he seemed more comfortable with her now that she was in her old clothes. She wondered what that meant.

Quickfoot and the other unicorns were still waiting for them outside. "What now?" asked Quickfoot. "More travelling?"

"Yes," Carla answered, "more travelling. We have to go visit the Dwarves."

Lungand spoke up then. "Bruderic, I think it would be for the best to go back to, or at least through, the kingdom. Let your people know that you are still alive."

"The quest to the Dwarves---"

"Will still be there if you take an extra three days to pass through Vorholm. Notice, I am not suggesting that you give up the quest. I am only suggesting that you limit the chance of trouble in the kingdom by showing yourself."

Bruderic shot a glance at Wissagebreht, who was carefully showing nothing in his face. Finally, he nodded.

"Yes, there is sense in that. Unless Wissagebreht objects too severely, we will do that."

Wissagebreht merely nodded.

Quickfoot said, "We unicorns cannot go into Vorholm yet; the Elves have not yet lifted the ban. We will go as far as the border, then meet you again on your way out."

"Why?" asked Carla. "You have brought us to the Elves, you need go no further."

The unicorn chuckled. "Mere curiosity, my dear. None of the three of us have seen the Dwarves, and I have an urge to do so."

"Well I, for one, will be glad of your company."

There were a pair of Elves there as well, armed and armoured, who were to escort the travellers to the edge of the forest. They did so quietly, speaking only when spoken to, and then only directly to the question. There was no friendly joshing as between fellow travellers. Though they shared meals with the party, the Elves did so without particular friendliness.

As with the trip in, it took a full day and part of another before they were on the edge of the wood. Once the travellers had gone out into the clearing, their two escorts, turned and, again, without a word of leavetaking, the two Elves disappeared into the woods. By this time, though, none of the four had expected any more.

Chapter 6

SEEKING THE DWARVES

By the middle of the next day, they had reached the edge of the small stream, just a little further down from where they had first met Quickfoot and his companions. Which was determined as part of the border of Vorholm. The unicorns bade the four farewell, and watched them as they marched on. Carla began to practice more intensely with her sling.

Shortly after they passed over the stream, Lungand said, "We should go to the castle of Lord Wyrgenhelm. He is nearest to our path, and we can get horses there. Not to mention letting it be known that the King is alive."

"Do you think that will be safe?" asked Wissagebreht.

"Wyrgenhelm is a man who, though he fancies himself as important, has not the courage to do anything drastic, such as attack his own king. We will be as safe there as anywhere."

By midafternoon they had hit the road which led, among other places, to the castle of Wyrgenhelm. They continued down that road dotted with trees. There were the occasional wagon paths leading off to farmlands. As they progressed towards the castle, Carla continued to practice with her sling. She was now picking marks and casting at them, developing her accuracy as she practised hitting large rocks and trees as they passed by on the trail. With a proper trail to follow, they were able to move somewhat faster and had covered a good deal of distance before evening.

In the morning they moved on, and in a short time were coming in sight of a castle. It was not much of a castle, though at the time Carla had little to compare it to. There was an inner keep, and five towers around the walls. From the keep flew a pennon, the She-wolf's head on a yellow background, signifying that the Lord of the Castle was in residence. The walls at a distance had seemed forbidding. But, closer inspection, revealed stones which had fallen out of place. Whole sections of wall were bulging at the base as the weight of stone and the effects of winter frost began to cause the wall to fall.

All around the outside of the castle was a town, mostly consisting of huts of the sort that Carla had lived in. There were one or two slightly better seeming houses, and a great many shops and vendors. If she had seen it before she had seen Drefcwed, the Elves' city, Carla felt sure that she would have been greatly impressed.

Carla had already put her sling away. But Wissagebreht said to her, quietly, "Best not practice with the sling in the sight of the guards of the castle or their Lord. Such people feel a little uneasy about weapons in the hands of such as we."

She nodded.

Bruderic surveyed the castle as they came closer. "It would not be proper now, when we are going to ask Wyrgenhelm for help. But when the quest is over remind me to send him a message regarding the upkeep of his castle, Lungand."

The Chamberlain nodded.

They walked the road toward the castle, passing through the town. From all Carla could see, it was less of a town than many she knew, and she wondered at the temporary nature of the buildings. Wissagebreht answered her unspoken question. "It is unlawful to have buildings outside the castle walls; they might be used against the castle in a siege. Every so often, the Lord of the castle must send his soldiers out to tear down and burn the buildings and drive the people out. Most of the people come back in a week or two and build again, but in such a case, who would bother to build a proper house?"

At the gate of the castle, two guards lounged about, leaning on spears. They were slowly surveying the people around with expressions of bored dismissal. As the four made their way to the gate, the guards' eyes fixed on them. They could see the guards taking in their dress, and the fact that two of them bore swords. Suddenly there was little of the boredom left on the guard's faces.

Lungand stopped in front of them. "We must talk to Lord Wyrgenhelm. I am the Lord Chamberlain Lungand, and this is King Bruderic."

The first guard, looking at them in disbelief, sneered, "Yes, and I'm Queen Guendatha come back to demand vengeance. Be off, then or---"
The other guard was hissing urgently in his ear. Something to the effect that he had seen the Chamberlain at court and this was he. The first guard paled, swallowed, and tried to speak. Lungand addressed the second guard.

"Escort us to your Lord."

"Yes, Milord."

Himself very pale, the guard marched along before them toward the keep.

Carla heard Bruderic mutter. "That guard is an ignorant boor, Lungand, but I do not want you to demand any punishment for him. It will be punishment enough for him to wait a few days in anxiety about his fate."

The Chamberlain merely nodded.

Wyrgenhelm was a slender dark-haired man with, it seemed, a perpetually worried expression. He had dark hair, watery eyes and a huge moustache which, on his small face, looked somewhat ridiculous. "Your Highness, Milord, this is a surprise. I had no idea you were coming."

A bolder man might have made a plain statement at the discourtesy of giving him no prior warning.

Bruderic spoke. "I presume that you have heard that we have been on a quest to seek out the reason why the unicorns do not return?"

"Why, yes, Highness, we had heard that."

"The quest is not yet ended. There is yet a thing to be done, and it is I who must do it. I regret being able to give you no warning of our coming. But we did not know ourselves until just lately that we would be coming this way, and it was not possible to send anyone ahead.

"But I must ask a few favours of you."

"Whatever I can do, I will, Highness."

"We need your hospitality for the night. We need horses to carry us further on the way. And we need a swift messenger to be sent to the capital to bring word of the situation to the Lords reigning for me."

The Lord was nodding as the King spoke, and when he had finished, Wyrgenhelm said, “Of course, of course. Please, let me have some refreshments sent for. You have been travelling a long while on foot, I can see."

"The message first, Lord, then the refreshments."

A moment later King Wyrgenhelm had sent a servant for paper, pen and ink, then he sent another servant for refreshments. The servant with the refreshments arrived while the King was in the process of writing out his message. Since Wyrgenhelm had no notion of the status of Wissagebreht and Carla. Save that they had arrived with the King and Chamberlain. he assumed that they were due the same courtesy, despite their looks.

Wine was served, a surprisingly good wine, along with small cakes which were also quite good. When Bruderic had finished his message, folded it, and given it to the messenger with instructions for delivery. He also took a cup of wine and a cake. Wyrgenhelm sat almost literally on the edge of his seat. He was fearful lest the least thing done or left undone should attract the notice of the King. Bruderic, on the other hand, strove to put him at ease by discussing all manner of harmless subjects. At last, Wyrgenhelm suggested that quarters be found for the four. Bruderic agreed, and they were soon in a set of rooms in the north part of the keep.

It was not possible to leave that same afternoon. Not if courtesy was to be maintained. But Bruderic made it clear that they would have to leave the next morning. They dined with the Lord and his chief officers that evening. Once again in borrowed clothing, and once again Carla noticed Bruderic looking at her.

Being King, Bruderic had to be seated at the head table and Lungand was with him. Wissagebreht and Carla were seated at lower tables among the knights and ladies. Wissagebreht was seated across the table from her. On her left was a young knight, named Aelinth, who paid lavish attention to her.

As the evening went on, he became bolder and bolder, and more free with his hands. Finally, Wissagebreht leaned across the table toward him. "Aelinth, you have not been properly introduced to my ward, Carla. She has been under my protection since she was born. A fortunate thing for a child, to have a Wizard's protection, don't you think?"

Aelinth looked at Wissagebreht and turned pale. The startled youth suddenly devoted his whole attention to his food.

After the meal, Bruderic sought Carla out. "I noticed that fool Aelinth pestering you. I have a mind to talk with him myself, perhaps introduce him to better manners."

"You needn't bother. Wissagebreht warned him off."

"But still---"

"Still nothing! Wissagebreht is my guardian! It is for him to protect me, not you!"

Bruderic shrank back, then smiled. "Ah, but I am your King, and have a responsibility to protect you, as well as all my subjects. But if you insist, I will do nothing more. For this time."

He bowed and turned away, leaving Carla still wanting to shout something at him. But she was not quite sure whether she thought he was a mere pest or a caring friend.

In the early morning they were riding out of the gate of the castle. The road stretched long and white ahead of them, and the day promised to be fair. Indeed, they had good travelling, and made very good progress towards the capital that day. In the morning, it suddenly occurred to Bruderic that the men-at-arms who were waiting at Wissagebreht's hut should be informed that they need not wait there any longer. He had therefore had a special messenger sent off to tell them.

They reached the capital the next evening, without incident. As they went in the main gate, Carla saw a man leap on a horse and ride up the main street as though his life depended on it. She remarked on that, and Bruderic said, "Yes. That will be a messenger taking word of our arrival to the Regents. They would not wish to be caught off-guard at the return of the King. Watch; they will have a huge party out to greet us."

He proved correct. As the rode into the palace courtyard, there were two rows of men-at-arms in polished armour. They stood like statues with spears held upright in right hands, shields on left arms. Down the way between the two rows the travellers rode, up to the knot of people who waited at the last step of the palace.

As they approached, all of people went down on one knee. Bruderic spoke. "Rise, faithful servants."

The people came to their feet. A certain few of them, clearly assigned the task beforehand, came to hold the horses while the travellers dismounted. Bruderic came over to Carla quickly and extended a hand to help her down.

She snorted, and jumped down, ignoring him. She stumbled, almost falling. When he caught her arm to steady her, she was all the more angry. But she decided it would be better not to make too much of a fool of herself in front of so many people. She smiled at him, and Bruderic turned to speak to the Regents.

"Good day, Milords. May I present you to the rest of my company? Lord Volkenor, Lord Nechtgang, these are the Wizard Wissagebreht and his ward, Carla.", Announced Bruderic.

Volkenor was old, not, extremely old, but older than Lungand, and somewhat stout. There was a young page with him whose duties included standing by and letting the Lord lean on his shoulder whenever he must bow. His face was round and brown, with black beard and eyebrows. Only a ruff of pepper-and-salt hair was left round the bald crown of his head. There was something about his eyes that Carla didn't trust, though she could not quite put words to it.

Nechtgang looked even older; he was thin and spare, with a full head of white hair and a white beard as well. When he moved, it could be seen that all his joints were stiff. His eyes were bright and clear, though, and when he spoke it was clear that age had not dimmed his thoughts. In him, Carla could feel something of old bitterness. He appeared to be a man who felt that for ages he had been denied his rightful due in the world.

Volkenor spoke first. "Wissagebreht I have met before. I welcome you back to the court, Wissagebreht. As for the young lady," he took her hand and bowed over it, only a slight bend of the back, "she is indeed a charming addition."

Nechtgang gave a quick sideward glance of disgust at his co-regent and himself bowed over Carla's hand. "I too know Wissagebreht, and I am pleased to make the acquaintance of his ward. Shall we go inside where we can be more comfortable?"

They went inside to the throne room. Volkenor said, as they were about to enter, "Milord King, you have had a long journey; would you not wish to wash up before you take your throne again?"

"No, Milord Volkenor, I have no time. I shall be here only the night, then I must go fulfill the last part of the quest."

The two of them looked at Bruderic together, hesitated, and then went on into the throne room. The throne was set up on a raised dais, and two smaller seats had been set up at the foot of the dais. Sincc the Regents could not possibly aspire to the throne. The Regents did not take these seats this time, however, but rather stood facing the throne to wait until the King should seat himself.

When he had done this, he looked down at the two. "Have there been any difficulties raised in my absence. Difficulties which were beyond your capabilities?"

They answered, almost simultaneously, "No, Milord."

"Good. Since we will be going out again in the morning, I would prefer to spend the night resting."

"You will eat with us, Milord King?" asked Volkenor.

"Certainly."

In all this time, Carla kept noticing the Wizard Gaistferu moving around the crowd of courtiers. His eyes always slipping from one to another of the powerful people. She remembered Wissagebreht's assessment of him. She then wondered what might happen if his ambition someday overpowered his fear.

In the morning, as Bruderic promised, after they gathered provisions and new mounts, they set out again. The trip went well, with no particular incident. Carla continued to practice with her sling, now from horseback. She was now able to hit a stone about the size of a man's head six times out of ten at a distance of twenty yards, from a moving horse. Wissagebreht watched, and when she looked at him after a good shot, he smiled at her.

Lungand remained grimly silent. Carla asked Wissagebreht, "Has he not yet accepted that this quest must be fulfilled?"

Wissagebreht smiled, a little sadly. "He has, or he would voice his objections. It is only that he wishes it were not necessary, wishes that they could stay in the Kingdom."

"He still feels that someone will rise up against the King while he is away?"

"Yes. There is less danger of that now, since we have come back through to show that the King still lives. That he has not disappeared off the face of the earth. But there is still some chance that some leader will find it possible to gather enough force to make the attempt."

"And if an attempt is made, it seems doubtful that the Regents could do much about it?"

He shook his head. "Don't mistake the Regents. They are both proven men on the battlefield, and fully experienced in the ways of convincing others into a wise course of action. Or, at least against an unwise course."

Carla shook her head in mystification. "Then why should Lungand be so concerned?"

The Wizard grinned. "Firstly, because Lungand trusts very few arrangements in the Kingdom unless he is himself present to oversee them. And secondly, because he fears that either or both of the Regents may suddenly realize that if the other Regent were to die. He would be well on the way to supplanting the King."

"Then we should perhaps not go---"

Wissagebreht waved a hand. "You may remember how Bruderic chose the two. Neither of them trusts the other, and each will be greatly concerned about any plot by the other. I do not plan to dawdle on this trip, for I recognize the dangers. But then again, what we do is something that must be done, and if there are risks, they must be taken."

On the second evening out of the capital Bruderic looked across the fire at Wissagebreht. "We are in much the same situation as when we went to the Elves, are we not? For the Dwarves live under the mountains, and it is said that a Man rarely sees a Dwarf who does not wish to be seen. How do we talk to the Dwarves, then?"

Wissagebreht smiled. "I have had dealings with the Dwarves from time to time. There is a door I know of, and hopefully there will be someone around to answer when we come knocking."

The foothills were considered beyond the territory of Vorholm. So, as they entered the foothills, the unicorns rejoined them. They had apparently been concealed in a small copse, for as the travellers went along, suddenly the unicorns were there.

Yssagarit trotted up to Carla and rubbed his muzzle on her leg. "I see you have new mounts; my companions and I wish you to know that you were not that heavy." There was laughter in his voice.

"Ah, it is good to see you again, Quickfoot! But be truthful now; did you not find us at least a little heavy?"

"Well, perhaps a little."

As they continued on in the foothills Carla could eventually see the mountains from afar and wondered at their blue aloofness. The party soon approached the trail to the mountains and Carla stared in awe by their sheer size. Never had she seen anything so tall. The mountains even dwarfed the largest castles. Carla gazed in wonder at the white caps on the highest of the mountains, and how some of them even reached up into the clouds. She had asked Wissagebreht about them, and he seemed to know at least a little about everything. So she now knew something about the mountains and what went on in them.

The trip became more arduous, for they had to climb. To climb, ever going upward. It would have been possible to ride all the time. But in order not to wear the horses out completely, they walked from time to time, leading the animals.

It grew cooler also, as they went upward. On their second day in the mountains Wissagebreht smilingly produced heavy fur garments which he had quietly procured in the capital during their brief stay. From the look on the face of Lungand it was clear that packing warm garments had completely slipped his mind, even though he had known where they must go.

"Fortunately," said the Wizard, "we are travelling in summer, and hence need not fear the winter storms. What we must beware of, however, is the possibility of avalanche."

"What is an avalanche?" inquired Carla.

"When huge masses of snow, ice, dirt, and rocks break loose from the mountain and slide down, carrying everything before them. There is something about the weather in spring which makes them more likely to happen at that time, and in summer only a little less so. The path I intend to take is one where such snowslides are not likely to happen. But 'not likely' does not mean 'impossible.'"

They saw one avalanche, far away. As they were plodding slowly up the mountain slope, with a fair green valley to their left, Wissagebreht suddenly spoke. "Look!"

They looked to where he was pointing, across the valley and upward. There had been a heavy overhang of snow there, and just before he pointed it had broken off and fallen to the slope. It began to slide, picking up speed, and as it went it pushed up more snow before it, which increased the force of it. The sound of it eventually reached them across the distance, a continuous roaring.

Then it hit the first of the trees, burying some under the snow, snapping off others and carrying them along, until the slope began to level off. By then the force of the slide was so terrific that much of the debris continued to move, almost all the way down to the valley floor.

"When the conditions are right, even a loud noise can suffice to start the snow sliding," said Wissagebreht.

The other three looked in silence at the devastation that had been wrought.

It was not much longer until they were up beyond the level where trees still grew. For a while, there were thin and scrawny bushes. They were tough little things anchoring themselves in tiny pockets of earth on the mountain's rocky face. There were also little patches of tough grasses which the horses did not like. But which they ate, for want of anything better.

"Forbidding country for anything to live, man, beast, or Dwarf," commented Lungand.

"Ah, the Dwarves do not commonly live this high; they prefer the lower areas, just as men do. But the entrance through which they welcomed me was high up, and perhaps for that same reason. No one would come this high without good and overriding cause."

"So they feared you might spread the word of this door to everyone?"

"Let us say rather that they were very cautious. The treasures of the Dwarves are legendary, and what might happen if the wrong sort of people knew of doors that gave easy access to those treasures?"

For some reason, the less hospitable the country, the more the unicorns liked to gambol and play. Even Lungand had difficulty not smiling when they went into their three-cornered dance in the evening.

It was afternoon of the next day when they came upon a small rock overhang, not unlike any number of similar formations they had seen previously.

"Ah, here we are!", declared Wissagebreht.

The others looked around for any sign of Dwarves, indeed, for any sign that anyone had ever been there. Beneath the overhang was the face of a great boulder, somewhat convex in shape, but no sign of a door anywhere.

"You are sure?" asked Lungand.

"Of course I am sure!" said Wissagebreht. "And of course you cannot see anything; I did tell you it was a secret door. How could it remain secret very long if it could be seen so easily?"

"So what do we do now? Knock?"

The Wizard raised his eyebrows. "As good a notion as any."

He took up his staff and rapped on the rock. There was no reaction.

Wissagebreht waited.

"Well?" demanded Lungand. "What now?"

"I expect we are being surveyed. Dwarvish doors very frequently include cunningly fashioned spy holes. This is so that they can look at those who demand admittance before they admit them."

"And for how long do we expect them to survey us before they admit us? And if they decide not to admit us, what then?"

"You worry too much, Lungand." But nevertheless, Wissagebreht took up his staff again and rapped once more on the door. There was still no answer.

Lungand merely looked at the Wizard. Meanwhile, Bruderic, who had thought only of coming to the Dwarves to fulfil the quest but had not thought that it might be difficult to arrange a meeting with the Dwarves, looked on in consternation.

Wissagebreht shrugged. "I would truly prefer to do nothing drastic, though I am prepared, if it should come to that. Let us camp here. If we have no sign of Dwarves by morning, I shall try something else."

Lungand's look showed how little he liked this, but he said nothing. He maintained his grimly disapproving look throughout the evening. He even seemed to maintain that expression after he went to sleep. Carla, who had great trust in Wissagebreht, wondered how long the Wizard would put up with this. She then began to wonder if Lungand's face had possibly set for good in a disapproving expression. This caused her to giggle, and she had to avoid telling either Wissagebreht or Bruderic the cause of her mirth.

In the morning the Chamberlain's disapproving expression was, if anything, stronger. After they had breakfasted, cleaned up the dishes, and packed their things, Wissagebreht once again rapped with his staff on the rock.

There was an almost inaudible scraping sound, and a large part of the boulder swung inward. In the doorway stood a Dwarf, shorter than Carla, broadly built, with strong arms and fingers. His face was broad, brown, weathered, and covered from the nose downward with a curling brown beard. There was a short sword slung at his left side. A dagger at his right, and he wore a plain brown smock over a pair of grey hose, and a pointed brown leather cap on his head.

He bowed. "Good morning to you, Wissagebreht," he said.

"Good morning. You have been watching us all night?"

"No. There is no regular watch at this door, but a patrol goes by regularly. Last night's patrol reported a party camping here, and I was sent with a small party to watch and see if it was merely chance travellers, or someone come to pay a call. So here I am, and here you are. What do you wish with the Dwarves?"

Wissagebreht frowned. "Do we discuss such matters on the doorstep?"

The Dwarf answered the frown with one of his own. "We let none in here without good reason. You may tell me here at the doorstep why you wish to be admitted, and I decide if that is sufficient reason."

Carla could feel Lungand's face becoming a thundercloud, but Wissagebreht was calm. "I am here with the King of Vorholm, his Chamberlain, and my ward, Carla. The King wishes to have a memorial made to the late Queen Guendatha."

Chapter 7

DUMBERLIN'S FORGE

The Dwarf's eyes widened slightly, but he showed no other sign of surprise. Carla, remembering her feelings on meeting the two Regents, felt that she was here looking at a solid wall of the same stone which made up the mountains.

"So? Well, I am permitted to make decisions as to whether those who seek to enter here do so for serious or frivolous reasons. I must say that this does not sound frivolous. Enter, then."

He stepped out of the way and allowed them to come in, horses and all. The unicorns at first looked doubtful, but then decided to enter too. Inside was a fairly plain sort of porch, with the walls carved into friezework depicting Dwarves at work in various forms of metal and stonework.

There were also thirty Dwarves as well, armed and armoured, carrying sword or axe and shield. They looked on the travellers with suspicion, and on the unicorns with wonder.

The first Dwarf spoke again. "My name is Vashchi. I will escort you down towards the King's suite. Whether or not he will see you is another matter entirely."

Wissagebreht nodded. "I am the wizard Wissabreht, as you know." He indicated the others, one at a time, with waves of his hand. "I present here the King, Bruderic of Vorholm, his Chamberlain, Lungand, and my ward, Carla."

The Dwarf bowed politely. "Pleased to make your acquaintance, I am sure. Shall we go?"

"What of the horses?"

"Tether them here, with the unicorns. Someone will come to see that they are fed while you are our guests."

Carla could feel Yssagarit tensing at these words. "The unicorns are not to be tethered!" she said, surprising herself with her firmness. "They come and go as they will, and are not to be tied."

Vashchi looked at her in surprise, then looked at her again, closely. Again, she could not read his expression, but there was something strange in it. He nodded. "So be it. The unicorns may come with us."

So they tethered the horses in the porch, and began walking. Some of the Dwarves carried torches. This was mostly as a courtesy to the visitors. For the Dwarves were capable of finding their way through every hole and cavern in the mountain without the aid of light.

They first made their way through a series of crude tunnels and steps which had been chiseled out of the rock. As they made their way further, the passages and stairs gradually became more smoothly and carefully crafted. They finally came to halls and stairways which were decorated by friezework of amazing skill and were lighted by lamps every so often along their length.

The scenes depicted on the walls were from various spheres of Dwarvish life and from various events in Dwarvish history. Carla longed to stop and ask about this one and that one, but did not quite dare.

She then noticed something about the lamps. At first, she had thought they were simple oil lamps. But then she saw that they were instead metal holders for gleaming jewels. Jewels which held light at their centre and shed it on the path. She could not contain her curiosity at this. "Wissagebreht!" she whispered, "What are those lights?"

"They are the Lamps of the Dwarves. No one knows how the light is held in them, for that is one of the secrets which the Dwarves do not sell, not for any amount of money."

Vashchi eventually led them into a spacious room with a number of benches in it. "If you will wait here, I will take word of your presence to the King."

He bowed and left them.

Bruderic looked around, then went to the door and looked out. "They must trust us greatly; there is no one guarding the door."

Wissagebreht smiled. "Why bother? We could easily find our way back up to the door through which we entered, but what of it? And if we, or any of us, went blundering about looking for treasure, we would be noticed, and guards called rapidly. Furthermore, they know the byways and passages of this place much better than we. So that even if we managed to steal something and get onto the right passage to the door, they would easily head us off and ambush us."

Bruderic grinned. "You need not fear, Wissagebreht, I had no thought of thievery."

The walls of this room were also decorated with scenes from Dwarvish life and history. So ornate were they that the conversation eventually turned to these scenes. Wissagebreht, surprisingly, knew most of the tales behind the scenes depicted. He was therefore able to tell the other three some interesting stories. Even Lungand, for lack of anything better to do, paid attention.

He was ending the tale of Daghuwerand. Who bought from the Dwarves the chains which he used to chain the dragon Allefallend, when Vashchi came back. "Which ending do you put to the tale, Wissagebreht? The one which says that the Dwarves, learning of how much gold was in the dragon's hoard. Demanded from Daghuwerand more than the agreed price. And when he would not pay, they cursed the chains they had made so that the chains broke. And the hero had to slay the dragon and died in doing so? Or, the one which says that Daghuwerand himself, seeing the riches in the dragon's hoard. Tried to cheat the Dwarves of their rightful due. And that it was this faith breaking which caused the chains to break?"

Wissagebreht looked up. "Why, as to that, I had planned to do what you have just done, to tell them both endings and let them judge for themselves. But since you have told the two endings of the tale, I need not bother."

Vashchi was still frowning. "Yes," he said, almost as though the Wizard had not spoken. "Years upon countless years ago it has been, yet the Dwarves have long memories."

"Indeed," answered Wissagebreht in a voice which was carefully neutral.

Vashchi looked up again, as though remembering something. "I beg your pardon, I forget my manners. The King will see you now."

He led them down more hallways until they came to a wide cavern, well-lit with the Dwarvish lamps. At the rear of which was a throne at the top of nine steps. The King of the Dwarves sat on that throne, but he had no sceptre in his hand, rather he held upright a double-bladed axe. They approached the throne, and bowed at the foot of the nine steps.

"Milord King, I present to you these travellers come with a request for the Dwarves. Bruderic, King of Vorholm, Lungand his Chamberlain, Wissagebreht the Wizard, and Carla, ward of the Wizard. Travellers, I present you to His Majesty, King Goral of the Dwarves."

The King looked down on them. He was old, old even as the Dwarves count years, with white hair and beard on a wrinkled brown face. His eyes were bright, though, and he surveyed them all carefully. At last he spoke.

"Why do you come here, King of Vorholm?"

"I come to commission the making of a memorial to the late Queen Guendatha."

King Goral nodded. "A very brief answer, King Bruderic. And yet Queen Guendatha has been dead these sixteen years; why a memorial for her now, suddenly?"

"It is a task laid on me by the Elves, in return for which they will remove the curse from our land. The Queen died in strange circumstances. Perhaps she was even murdered, and because of this the Elves have cursed the fertility of our land."

The Dwarf-King nodded, as though he were merely confirming what he already knew. "The revenge of the Elves can be frightening, can it not? But what sort of memorial had you in mind?"

"They had suggested, and I accept their suggestion, that the manner and form of the memorial be left to your craftsmen."

Again the King nodded. "And what are you willing to pay?"

"Keeping in mind that the payment will come out of my own resources, and not from those of my Kingdom, I will pay whatever is reasonable."

"Hmm. Perhaps your own weight in gold?

"'Whatever is reasonable,' I said, not every penny that I own or could hope to own. One quarter of that."

"Three quarters."

"One third."

At this point Vashchi broke in. "Your Highness, may I make a suggestion?"

The King, an expression of annoyance on his face, said, "What is it, Vashchi?"

The Dwarf went quickly up the steps to the throne and whispered briefly into the ear of the King. The King sat up straighter and smiled. "Indeed, the very thing." He turned his face to the travellers.

"King Bruderic," he continued, "Vashchi has just reminded me of something which might take the place of payment. A small task which requires valiant people to carry it out."

"And what is that task?" asked Bruderic, cautiously.

"To watch the forge of Dumberlin for one night."

Bruderic lifted an eyebrow. "It sounds altogether too simple to be payment for such a memorial. What is the trick here?"

"No real trick," answered the King. "The forge of Dumberlin is the forge at which we make most of our special works. Those with particular spells or made with certain materials. Because of that there is always a hint of magic about the place, which tends to draw certain creatures to it.

"Many of these creatures are mere pests, capable only of hindering the work which goes on in the forge. But there are others which are more deadly. Those who guard the forge therefore, must be people of valor. They must be people who are able to stand against strangeness without flinching."

"Before I say yes or no, let me consult with my companions."

The King nodded. "Certainly. Do you wish to come back later with your answer?"

"No, I think if we merely withdraw to a quiet corner for a moment, we can make our decision."

"Very well."

So they moved aside, against a wall where a huge and fearsome dragon was carved. Then Bruderic looked at Wissagebreht. "Wissagebreht, I am willing to make decisions about things if I know all the facts. In this case, I know practically nothing. Can you advise me?"

"Until Vashchi reminded him of the forge, I think he would have been willing to make an agreement for money. Now, though, I fear that he may well insist on this task, or perhaps one as hard. It has taken his fancy to see the King of Vorholm work for him."

"Indeed? But what of this forge? How dangerous is it? Is it too much of a risk?"

"It is a risk. However, just as the King said, it is not possible to predict just what must be guarded against. If all that come are the pests he mentioned, then you may well have your memorial at a cheap price. If something more dangerous should appear, then the memorial may cost you more than you might be willing to pay."

Lungand spoke. "If you take my advice, Bruderic, you will refuse. The Dwarves have little love for us, that is obvious, and it is quite possible that this is merely a trap to kill you."

Bruderic shook his head. "I doubt that. Most likely it is as Wissagebreht and the King seem to say. A task which could be dangerous, very dangerous, but not necessarily fatal. I intend to accept the conditions."

"So, then," said the Wizard. "In such a case, since my advice has led you to accept this task, I shall accompany you to give you what aid I can."

Bruderic nodded and, despite Lungand still looking like a thundercloud, approached the throne once more. "Milord King Goral, we will accept the task."

"'We'?" inquired the King of the Dwarves. "Did I ask that all of you take part?"

"No, but then neither did you say who or how many should, and Wissagebreht wishes to join me."

"And I too," said Carla, hardly believing it was her voice speaking.

"And I also," said Lungand. "Since we are all being fools, I should be one as well."

King Goral merely nodded, but he looked at Carla. "Carla, daughter of the Elves, do you truly wish to do this? Is it your quest?"

"Milord King," said Carla, a little surprised that he knew of her connection to the Elves, "It is my quest. I have been a part of it since it began, and I feel it would be hardly right to separate myself from it now."

He nodded again. "So, then. I shall put the matter of the memorial to my craftsmen, and in the meantime you will be shown to guest quarters. Tonight you shall go to Dumberlin's forge."

The Dwarves were as free in their hospitality as the Elves. The main difficulty was that the entertainers. The harpers and the Dwarves who acted out small plays, did so mainly in the Dwarvish language. So the four were unable to understand most of it. Out of courtesy, however, King Goral did order some songs to be sung in the language of Vorholm. It was in this way that they were not completely left out.

One great difference was that the Dwarves did not have clothing on hand to fit the travellers. So they were required to come to the table in their travelling dress. Carla felt a little uncomfortable about this and noticed the Bruderic was feeling somewhat the same. But as the evening went on they both managed to put those feelings aside and enjoy themselves.

When the evening's meal and entertainment were over, they were escorted back to their quarters to wait for the summons to the forge.

Yssagarit wished to come along with them to the forge. Carla, however, said, "No. This is something dangerous, and it is part of our quest, not yours."

"And if we come anyway?"

Carla looked around helplessly at Wissagebreht. The Wizard smiled. "Quickfoot, while we would like to have your company, I fear that it would not be safe, not for any of us. Please wait here for us."

"And if we say no?"

Wissagebreht frowned. "In such a case, I should have to lay a spell of binding on you, and neither you nor I should like that. Will you stay?"

"Oh, very well, then.", The unicorn snorted and turned away. Then all three of them went as far from the four travellers as they could manage.

"Don't worry, Carla," said Wissagebreht. "They will come back, once they are over their temper."

The Dwarvish forges were usually mere areas in the caverns where they set up anvils and furnaces. Dumberlin's forge had been similar. Until, after a long time of making magical things, it began to attract strange forces and apparitions. One of the first attempts to deal with these strange happenings had been to erect a roof and walls about the forge. This had proven useful only to a very small degree and for a short time, but no one had bothered to remove the roof or walls.

At present, whenever the forge was to be used, armed and armoured Dwarves had to stand guard outside to keep away the things attracted by the magic. Some came out of curiosity, and were only nuisances which might get in the way at a time when the work inside required great care. Others were of the sort to play wicked little tricks on the smiths or anyone present. While others still, more wild and unpredictable, might attack those in the forge or nearby. Most of the lesser ones would be frightened away by the mere presence of guards. Others could be shooed off without great trouble. But some of them might well try to kill or injure.

All this information was passed to them by Vashchi as he guided them to the forge. He appeared to be quite merry about the whole thing, and seemed to cherish a small and barely concealed hope that things would go badly for them.

The forge appeared to consist of a squat stone house, with a roof of thin slabs of stone. There was a chimney at the furnace end, and smoke was already coming out of that. With a smile that was almost a smirk, Vashchi said, "A good night to you, and good fortune be with you."

The King of the Dwarves had sent shirts of chain-mail and shields to the four. Along with the message that he hoped these would be helpful during the night. Carla found the mail shirt to be heavy and uncomfortable. But when she suggested taking it off, Wissagebreht gave her a look which said that she was being foolish, so she left it on. She did, however, dispose of the shield as being too much of an interference with her sling.

For the first part of the evening, nothing happened at all. Carla was just about convinced that they would have no difficulty at all when she saw something white out of the corner of her eye. She turned her head, but it was gone.

Wissagebreht shook his head. "It is beginning."

Across the cavern, a pale greenish face began to appear on the wall. Its strange eyes surveyed the four, then it disappeared. A pack of shaggy black dogs with eyes like orange fire trotted out of nowhere and came toward the forge. The dogs then spotted the four and sat down on their haunches, with their tongues lolling out. Nothing attempted to attack them yet. But strange shapes appeared and glowered at them.

"Wissagebreht," asked Carla, "could you not drive these off with spells?"

"Why, I suppose I could. But the magic I used to drive them off would attract other, stronger things which would need stronger spells to drive them off. Until, in the end, the things which would come, would overwhelm us. Oh, I can use little spells to assist in the work, but nothing large. We must do this mostly without magic."

Something like a pale bat swooped down at them, fluttering back up into the darkness as Bruderic brought up his sword. It swooped back down again, but on the third time around, Carla was already swinging her sling. Once, twice, she whirled it round her head, then let go. The stone went straight through the batlike thing, scattering it into pale, cloudy chips which drifted to the ground and disappeared.

Slowly but surely, more and more strange creatures crept out of the darkness. There were more batlike creatures, some of them flew, some of them skittered or even hopped across the floor. Then came snakes which wriggled across the cavern floor toward them. There were also swarms of gnats, and many other such creepy-crawly and sometimes slithery things. None of them proved dangerous. A sweep of a sword, a stone from Carla's sling, a stroke from Wissagebreht's staff, and they were dissipated.

All this time the pack of dogs sat watching and waiting. Then they were given a brief respite. The dogs sat quietly watching them and waiting as the four panted for breath.

There was a clattering across the cavern floor and they looked up to see a pile of bones lying there. The bones moved, rattling together. Suddenly, there was a complete skeleton standing up and advancing toward them. Followed by another and another and another, nine in all.

Carla's heart pounded, and she wanted desperately to run from here, to find a hiding place until this night should be over. But Bruderic was standing fast, and Wissagebreht did not appear overly concerned, so she swung her sling again.

Her first cast missed badly. But her second one smashed full into the skull of one of the skeletons, knocking it free from the neck bone. The skeleton dropped, and began feeling around on the floor with bony fingers. Carla took up another stone.

Her next cast smashed ribs in one of the other skeletons. The next one she missed altogether. As she took up another stone, she saw that the first skeleton had found its skull and replaced it again, and had rejoined the advance. They were close now, and they reached out with bony hands towards the four.

As though at a signal, the three men stepped forward, striking. Carla swung her sling again and again, sometimes knocking a leg or foot or arm loose. But each time the skeleton would grope about for the missing part, replace it, and come on.

The men were having similar difficulties. Any skeleton which they cut down with a sword would grope about, reform its parts, rise slowly, and rejoin the fray.

Carla noticed something else, however. Bones which were broken did not knit, but remained broken. With all her force, she flung a stone, which shattered a skull completely. The skeleton fell and groped for the skull, but could not find it.

Lungand appeared to have discovered this by himself. For now, the ground before him was a litter of shattered bones. Bruderic, too had destroyed one skeleton, chopping until there were not enough whole bones to form and fight.

At that very moment, one of the last skeletons came directly toward Carla. She could no longer pay attention to the battle the others were fighting, but must fight her own fight. Her first stone missed altogether. But her second smashed some ribs and apparently knocked the spine out of place. The bony figure fell, writhed a little, and then began to rise. Carla was already whirling her sling, and let fly another stone.

This one smashed a shoulder. The skeleton staggered. Then it regained its balance and kept coming, groping for her. She backed up, but she no longer had space to swing her sling. She began reaching for her dagger. But at that moment, Bruderic stepped quickly sidewise. Brutally, he struck backhanded into the skeleton, smashing it to the ground. While it was down, he struck again and again, smashing the skull and several other bones.

He looked at Carla and grinned, but said nothing. She was angry at him for helping. Angry at herself for needing help. But she knew that she couldn't have fought the skeleton all alone, so she forced herself to smile at him.

None of the skeletons were still whole, but some of the bones were still moving on the ground. The party smashed and hacked at them until they seemed no longer dangerous. Then straightened and waited for what would come next.

The dogs still sat watching the four with their orange fire eyes. They had not long to wait. Shortly an armoured figure came marching across the cavern. The armour was rusty, in some places no more than a thin film of red. But the sword in its hand was bright, brighter than it should be, and there was something ominous in the sheen of it. The Helmet had a crown affixed to it. This crown matched the crown which had been painted on the shield. The shield seemed to have escaped the general rust and corrosion of the rest of the armour.

As it came nearer, Carla saw that there was no face under the helmet, only a grinning white skull. For some reason, it seemed even more frightening than the skeletons they had just disposed of.

They stood staring for a long time, until the figure had covered half the distance between them. Finally, Carla managed to bring herself into action. She swung the sling around her head and released a stone. The stone glanced off the rusty crown but did not cause the foe to stop or even slow.

She took another stone, calmed herself as best she could, and threw it. This one went into the bony eye-socket. This time the apparition checked its movement forward. The head turned slightly in her direction. When it began to move again, it was coming straight at her. She noticed briefly that the men had spread out a little further from her. Then there was nothing at all but the Skeleton King in rusted armour marching steadily toward her. She judged that she had time for one more stone before it was too close, and she whirled her sling again. She missed badly, and at that range she ought not to have missed. She took another step back, putting another stone in her sling.

It was useless, she knew, but she had to try. Then Bruderic was chopping at the Skeleton King from the right. Wissagebreht was striking at the figure from the left. With Lungand attacking from the rear. When the first blows fell on it, it turned to defend itself and raised its sword to attack.

It moved slowly. It raised its sword and struck so slowly that Bruderic was easily able to interpose his shield. Carla saw the shock on his face as the blow hit his shield, and he staggered back and went down on one knee.

The Skeleton King, however, was not able to take advantage of Bruderic's fall. For the other two had redoubled their attack on him. He turned again, striking at Wissagebreht. The Wizard, having seen what had happened to Bruderic, did not attempt to parry the blade with his staff. Instead, he skipped backward as the blade swept by.

By now Bruderic was up again, and moving in. The armour of the skeleton King was being battered to pieces now, but he still moved as well as ever. The men had discovered the way to attack was to step in and strike. Perhaps strike several times, until the King turned to them. Then they would move back fast. Quicker than the King could move, while the others were striking again at his back.

Carla suddenly realized that she had a stone in the sling and was doing nothing. Picking her moment, she cast her stone again. It glanced off the armour, with no effect.

They seemed to be making little progress. The King was still moving as well as ever. Despite gaping rents in his armour, and smashed bones of the skeletons on the floor. Carla continued to throw stones whenever there was an opening. While the others continued to strike and strike. Desperation on most of their faces now. Wissagebreht alone looked calm, his face only going grim as each blow of his staff landed.

Bruderic took a desperate risk, stepping in to choose his spot carefully and hewed at an armoured thigh. The King staggered a bit. But then he turned. As the King turned, he swung a backhand blow towards Bruderic. Moving back and ducking at the same time, then falling flat on his back, Bruderic barely avoided the blow. The King stepped forward, ignoring the others, to raise his sword and strike down again. Bruderic managed to roll aside just in time. Sparks flashed from the sword of the skeleton King striking the stone floor.

Now the King was no longer able to ignore the others, but turned to face them. Bruderic came to his feet again and stepped back into the battle. He began striking again at the same thigh, though not such a heavy blow. This time when the King turned on him he was able to dodge back more easily. Lungand suddenly appeared to realize what Bruderic was attempting. Then he also struck at the King's thigh. The Chamberlain was larger than Bruderic, and his blow fell heavier. The armour parted, as did the bone beneath.

When the King moved now, his right leg dragged, and it was much easier for the three men to avoid him. Again and again one of the men would strike at the King's thigh, and at last the armour parted and the leg fell away. The skeleton King fell sideward and rolled to his back.

But the battle was not over. The King still swung his sword at anyone in reach. Leaving the men to hew at his arms, leaping in and out quickly as he was facing someone else. When half his right forearm fell away, he dropped his shield and rolled to take up the sword in his left hand. He was swinging it with little less skill than he had shown with his right.

Without the shield to hinder them, the men were more able to move in and strike more easily. During all this time, Carla did not take part. The sling was no weapon for this sort of work, which required constant chopping until a bone gave way.

When the left arm fell away, the King continued to thrash about. Wissagebreht knelt suddenly beside him, out of reach of his severed left arm. Then he put a hand on his chest, and said something quietly. The skeleton subsided into stillness.

Bruderic recovered his breath enough to be curious.

"What was that?"

"I said, 'Be at rest, King.' in his language."

"You know him?"

Wissagebreht looked up. "I knew him. It is a long tale. If there were a time and place to tell it, I would. But this is neither."

His voice forbade questions. His eyes glittered for a moment, and Carla thought he was weeping. But he stood still.

"I thought you said you dared not use any spells," said Lungand.

The Wizard shook his head. "That was no spell. Not rightly, anyhow. How do we stand?"

Wissagebreht himself was unwounded. Bruderic had a small scratch on his right temple; Lungand had a more serious cut on his right forearm. After bandaging Lungand's arm, Wissagebreht looked at Bruderic's wound. By that time, it had already stopped bleeding. So the Wizard only wiped up the blood and declared him a fortunate young man.

Bruderic looked around. "How much longer do you think we have to wait?"

"It is past midnight. Before long, the worst of the danger should be over."

"If this was not the worst we can face, do you think we can survive?"

"If we do not allow ourselves to be defeated before the battle is fought. What would you do? Flee this fight and save your skin?"

Bruderic stiffened. "I am no coward!" His eyes blazed.

"Good. Early morning can make cowards of the best of us. If we stand here worrying about what may come next, we are likely to flee at the sight of a mouse."

There was a flat stone outside the door to Dumberlin's forge. So Lungand and Bruderic spent a few minutes doing what they could for honing the edges of their swords. The armour of the Skeleton King, though rusted and old, had still dulled and nicked the blades. While there was little to be done about the nicks, they could rectify the dullness.

For a long time, nothing happened. Then there was another crowd of the batlike things. Which were rapidly dissipated and driven off. During all this time the dogs still sat on their haunches and watched.

There was a shuffling sound over across the way where the wall was hid in shadows. Out of that darkness came a strange shape, then another, then another. They were tall. Taller than ordinary men, and they were wrapped in old, mouldering funeral shrouds. Their faces were covered, but they seemed not to need eyes to know where they were going. Carla, by main force, prevented herself from giving more than a tiny squeak. But she noticed that both Bruderic and Lungand were pale.

Wissagebreht spoke. "Hold fast! They can do naught to you if you stand up to them!"

Carla, still shivering with fear, whirled her sling and cast a stone. It smacked full into the chest of one of them, who stopped a moment, then advanced again toward her. Bruderic stepped forward, evaded a groping hand, and struck. The walking corpse, severely wounded, stopped and stepped back a pace. The other two halted beside it.

For a while, then, they stood facing each other, each group waiting for the other to move. A feeling of fear began to wash over Carla. A knowledge that if the walking corpses attacked, they could not be defeated. They were dead already; how can the dead be slain?

Wissagebreht spoke again. "Hold firm, all of you; the fear is a part of them, and if you give in to it, they will have won."

Carla focussed on what the wizard said. She managed to hold herself from running, but how, she never knew. The fear continued, however it was easier to fight now.

At last the walking dead stepped back, and back, and back. When they were beyond the row of watching dogs, they stopped and waited. The fear emanating from them was weaker at this distance, enough so that the four could stand it more easily.

Thus matters stood for some time. Nothing new came forth from the shadows, and Carla began to hope that perhaps the worst had passed.

There was a scraping and slithering in the shadows. Something which sounded as though several metal chains were being dragged across the stone floor. Then, into the light thrust a large greenish head. Followed by several feet of sinuous neck, then the body, and at last the tail. It was a dragon!

The jaws were about as long as Carla's arm. Its skin was covered with green scales. A pair of large rolling eyes were set back on its head. The body of the dragon was about the size of a horse. But there was nothing of the horse in that reptilian body. The long slender neck, or the tail which rolled and twisted for half again the length of the body. The four legs had clawed feet, and the claws tinked and chinked metallically on the stone floor.

The dragon did not breath fire. But something dripped from his fangs and when spots of it hit the floor, they smoked and hissed fiercely. The dogs seemed to sit up in anticipation.

Wissagebreht took a deep breath. "So. Now we see battle indeed."

Bruderic said nothing, merely hefted his sword and shook a kink, real or imagined, out of his shield-arm. Lungand muttered:

"Dwarves and dragons and dungeons dark!

Ye harpers, who sing of heroes, hark!"

It was all too much for Carla, and she wanted to run away, weeping. Wissagebreht spoke quietly. "Move out, now. We need room to face this foe. Like the Skeleton King, he can see only in one direction, but with fang and claw, he can strike out in several ways at once. And if he rises up on his hind feet, be careful not to let him fall on you!"

They were moving now, out and away from the forge, spreading out. Carla cast a stone from her sling. The stone hit the dragon's right shoulder and dropped away, unnoticed. 'So,' she thought, 'the body is invulnerable. What can I do?'

The head swung around, looking straight at her. Fear fell on her, and she was about to run when she felt Wissagebreht's hand on her shoulder. "There is no flight from this one. That is what he wants."

With the touch of the Wizard's hand, her fear lessened. Despite the huge eyes as large as dinner plates staring at her. That brought her an idea and she put a stone in her sling. Meanwhile, the dragon turned its attention to Bruderic, who was carefully advancing from its right. She swung the sling and cast and it seemed for a moment that it would go straight and true. Then the dragon struck like a serpent at Bruderic, its jaws opened wide. The stone went harmlessly over its head.

Bruderic just barely quickly enough, dodged aside. While at the same moment, Lungand was rushing in from the other direction. Who began striking at the armoured side. Carla in the meantime had taken another stone, and again she cast it. Again, just at the last moment, the dragon moved its head and the stone glanced harmlessly off its cheek.

The battle raged thus for some time. With the men moving in and striking. Then dodging the dragon's return blows of claw or tooth. Nor were they always completely successful. Lungand took a dreadful gash down his leg so badly that he could barely walk. Wissagebreht had to leave Bruderic to fight the dragon alone while he used some minor spells to stop the bleeding and begin the healing.

During this time, Carla finally managed to hit her mark. The dragon roared frightfully as the stone smashed its eye. He suddenly turned to this pest which had been flinging futile stones at him. It then leaped at her with a tremendous roar. She saw the white and pale green underside of the dragon coming down on her. Barely remembering Wissagebreht's warning in time, she turned and ran.

The stone floor shook under the weight of the beast, and Carla turned her head to see what had happened. It had come down just where she had been standing, and the head was striking out for her. She leaped forward, outdistancing the strike by a little. She would have kept going except that she ran into the wall of the forge.

She fell back from there, half-senseless, and only the sounds of fighting behind her forced her to her feet. When she got up, she found that Bruderic had run up to the prostrate dragon and thrust his sword into its side with all his force.

The worm threw back its head and gave a tremendous bellow, then turned to strike at the young King. Bruderic was dodging back already. But even that might not have saved him had not the loss of one eye hindered the dragon's co-ordination. As it was, in his haste to pull back Bruderic stumbled and fell. As he scrambled to his feet, the dragon bellowed again, then turned and began dragging itself away.

Lungand was striding forward purposefully, but Wissagebreht laid a hand on his arm. "Let be! He is leaving, let him go!"

Bruderic was now standing, looking at the sword in his hand. The blade was blackened and corroded, no edge to it at all. He laid it to the stone but at the first stroke, it broke, falling to powder as he stared at it.

Wissagebreht looked at it, then at Bruderic. "Dragon blood. Did you get any of that on yourself?"

Bruderic looked at his hands, then at his armour. There were a few splashes on his armour and in those spots, the metal was already falling to pieces.

"No, I think not."

"Good. It would be painful, at the very least."

Bruderic looked down at the remains of his sword. "What will I use for a weapon now?"

Wissagebreht chuckled. "That does you credit, young man. There are few who fight and gravely wound a dragon who come away so unscathed."

"But my sword!"

"You may not have noticed, but the night is over. At least, it is so nearly over that I doubt that we will see any further difficulty. Look!"

The dogs, who had sat there all night grinning at them, got up, turned, and trotted away.

"Then we have won!"

"Essentially so, yes. We have a little time to wait, though, so be patient."

Bruderic stood quiet a moment, then suddenly seemed to remember something.

"Uncle," he said to Lungand, "when the dragon came, that was the first time I remember you speaking poetry."

The Chamberlain thought for a while, not understanding. Then suddenly he realized what Bruderic had been referring to. He smiled, a little grimly. "As a boy, I learned a lot of poetry. In the past years, I have had little time to do so, but I have a good memory. And it seemed appropriate."

The Royal Dwarvish Company came out to the forge to survey the party. King Goral looked down on the four. With bright eyes, he was surveying the state of their armour. He looked over Lungand's leg, the bump on Carla's head where she had hit the wall, and Bruderic's empty scabbard. "It was a busy night, then?"

Wissagebreht nodded. "A busy night and I think we have well earned our wages."

"Oh, yes, I believe you have. Milord King of Vorholm, let me offer you our hospitality again. At least until you have rested yourselves."

Bruderic nodded. "I thank you, King Goral. And what of the memorial?"

King Goral smiled. "Now that is not something to be finished overnight. I promise delivery to you in your capital city in three weeks' time. Will that suffice?"

"It will suffice."

"Good. Then Vashchi will show you to your rooms. Rest well."

They rested for most of the day. In the evening, the King sent a new sword for Bruderic, along with a new mail shirt, and an invitation to come to dinner.

Dinner was good. Though the four were still tired enough that by the middle of it all of them were yawning. All save for Wissagebreht, who continued to regard everything around with mild amusement.

In the morning, they departed once more, with good wishes from the King and from Vashchi.

Chapter 8

REBELLION!

They made their way back down the mountains, the trip down being a little easier than that coming up. They had achieved their quest, and all their hearts were much lighter now. Lungand, in fact, told a few jokes from time to time, which surprised Carla very much. One evening after supper, Bruderic was even able to prevail upon Lungand, convincing him to recite to the party the whole of the poem. The very one which he had begun to recite when the dragon had appeared at Dumberlin's forge.

On the day that they came down out of the mountains into the hills, they saw a far-off plume of dust on the road. Lungand's face turned grim again. "A man only hurries like that if he bears important news. I fear that it will be bad news for us."

"Bad news?" asked Bruderic. "What sort of bad news?"

"It could be any number of things. But let us wait until the messenger himself appears before we borrow trouble."

Carla looked at Wissagebreht. She hoped that the Wizard would describe other reasons for a person to be hurrying along this particular path toward them. But even she had a fear in her heart that Lungand was right. And Wissagebreht was looking nearly as grim as Lungand.

Long before the rider came close enough to be identified, they could see sun glinting on helmet and armour, which meant a man-at-arms. For some reason this fact made Carla even more fearful.

At last he was close enough that they could see his face. It was Brehtand. As they drew closer, it became clear from his face that there was serious trouble ahead.

He spoke even as he came riding up. "Treachery, Milord King! Treachery and rebellion!"

"Calmly now, Brehtand. What is it?"

"Milord King. Nechtgang and Volkenor had begun plotting against each other from the day you first installed them as Regents. Last week Volkenor died, and it is suspected that he was poisoned. Three days later, the people who serve Nechtgang began to put it about that you have left the Kingdom alone for too long, and are no proper King. They do not say so, but the idea is left that Nechtgang would be preferable.

"Then Nechtgang called the people together in the Market Square. He began making a long speech about how the land needed a ruler of whom they could be certain. Not a boy who was serving at Lungand's every whim."

He glanced at the Chancellor at that point, but there being no interruption, he continued.

"While he spoke, the Wizard Gaistferu was standing behind him, overlooking the crowd. From time to time, he would say something to a scribe standing beside him, who wrote quickly. The next day, guards were sent out to arrest several people, Lords and leading citizens. Everyone who appeared to object to Nechtgang's plans. Rumour has it that the Wizard himself interrogates them, and often sends out guards to arrest others whom they mention.

"A few of those thus arrested have been executed, and some others released. But those who are released appear to have had their minds affected in some way. Much to the point that they are capable of little more than eating and sleeping.

"All this has made many who would otherwise be loyal to you either join Nechtgang or flee the city to avoid being taken."

"You came out alone?"

"Yes, Milord. Some of your loyal Lords, such as Malemergen, wished you to be warned, but dared not set out themselves. Nechtgang has them all watched, though there are some whom he dares not touch just yet. And that cursed Wizard is everywhere! Using his power or his mere presence to frighten those who would object."

"So, if Nechtgang is spreading doubts about my return, then it is likely that he will be seeking to insure that I do not return. Did you see any suspicious-looking people along the way here?"

"No, Milord, but they may have come out since I did."

Bruderic nodded. "We are fortunate that you got away so soon, Brehtand. If people have been sent out to guard against my return. They will almost certainly have orders to guard against anyone warning me. I think that before we go further we had best make some sort of plans. Uncle, have you any suggestions?"

"Only some obvious ones. You must show yourself as soon as possible, but you dare not show yourself alone. You will first have to go to one of your trusted Lords, and work from there. The problem, of course, is to pick a Lord whom you know for certain to be loyal. If the man is already a creature of Nechtgang or frightened by Gaistferu, you might well walk into a trap."

Bruderic nodded. "Malemergen would be best, but he is in the capital, under the eye of Nechtgang. Who is the nearest Lord who will be loyal to me?"

Lungand stared off into the sky thinking, and a moment later said, "Hergard is probably the best choice. He has enough force to protect us until we have gathered an army to fight."

"Fighting will be necessary?"

"I do not think that Nechtgang will quietly put aside all his claims simply because you appear again. Of course, if the people he has gathered desert him, then the thought of a battle is likely to lose its appeal."

"Let us go, then."

"Softly." The Chamberlain laid a hand on Bruderic's bridle. "We have already decided that he will have murderers out and waiting for you. If you ride into an ambush, all our planning will go for naught."

Bruderic relaxed himself a bit and nodded. "You are right, of course. Perhaps we should leave the trail altogether."

"Yes, since we could hardly scout every bush and hollow, I think we must. It will make our travelling slower, but safer."

As they began to move off the road, Yssagarit once again came up to Carla. "We are coming to Vorholm once again, and we cannot go there yet. But we hope to see you in the future."

"Good-bye Quickfoot," said Carla, "and thank you for your company and your assistance."

"No thanks are necessary. It is not many unicorns who have seen the city of the Elves, or who have been in the Caverns of the Dwarves."

With a switch of the tail, Quickfoot bounded away, followed by the others.

As they rode along, Carla managed to bring her mount beside Wissagebreht. "Wissagebreht, what does this mean? Must this war be fought? Can we win it?"

Wissagebreht shook his head. "Bruderic is the son of a man who took the throne with disputed legality. For that reason, throughout all his life there has always been the danger that some other Lord would see himself as being a better King. It has happened on several other occasions. But always the King and the Chamberlain were able to move quickly enough to prevent them from gathering support.

"As for your other questions, I am no seer, to tell the future. I can look at all the facts which come to hand and guess, but that is all. I fear the war must be fought. Nechtgang has had too much time to make his arrangements, to gather his forces and make promises to his followers. Some may drop away when the King declares himself and shows that he, too, has a following. But I doubt that those desertions will make much difference. Indeed, there will be many on our side slow to gather to our banner, waiting until things are more clear. And it is on such things which depend whether or not we can win this war."

With Brehtand scouting ahead, they carried on. Occasionally Lungand and Bruderic conversed. Speaking mostly in low voices, they discussed the strategy to follow. She herself caught only scraps of this conversation. Since it referred to Lords and knights who were mere names to her, she could not put forth much interest in it. They came at last to a castle built in a river valley, right up against the river. A ditch had been dug around the castle to surround the whole with water. As with Wyrgenhelm's castle, there was a large ramshackle village built outside the walls.

The castle was quite tall, but seemed to be in better condition than Wyrgenhelm's hold. There was, however, one section of a wall which had collapsed due to the weight of the stone on the wet ground. But there were workmen busily building that up.

Unlike the guards at Wyrgenhelm's castle, the guards here knew the King and the Chamberlain by sight. And so, they admitted the party readily, calling a messenger to take them immediately to the Lord Hergard.

Hergard was big and bearlike, with a shaggy head of red hair and an equally shaggy beard. For all his large and imposing size, he displayed a rough good humour. When he came to the King, he knelt, a sort of a bob of the knee, then straightened. There was no insolence in the gesture. It was more a recognition of the fact that they had a good deal to do and little time in which to do it.

"Welcome, Milord King! I had hoped that you would come to my castle first, though to be sure it is not in the best of repair."

Bruderic smiled. "I thank you for the welcome, Lord Hergard. And I hope that this business does not come down to a matter of holding sieges of castles. Hopefully we can bring Nechtgang to the battlefield and destroy him there.

"But before we go further, let me introduce my companions. Besides the Chamberlain, whom you already know. may I present the Wizard Wissagebreht and his ward, Carla."

Hergard gave Wissagebreht a searching look. "Welcome, Wizard. You have chosen to return to the court, then?"

Wissagebreht shrugged. "I left the court for a particular reason, as you know. The King came to me for help in healing the land, and the help meant a long quest. Because of the quest, Nechtgang and Gaistferu were able to plan and carry out their treachery. I feel that the least I could do is add my counsel to the King's cause."

The large man continued to look at Wissagebreht for a time, then smiled. "Good! I am sure that we will need all the counsel we can get. We will also need every sword we can bring to our cause; have you any counsel as to that?"

"I might have some suggestions about that, yes. But we have had a long ride; can we not find somewhere to sit down as we discuss this?"

"Of course! What a fool I am to keep you standing here. Come, come, this way!"

He led them quickly to a room with several chairs and benches, and a table in the middle with a map on it. Somewhere along the way he must have given a signal to somebody. Though Carla could not remember seeing it. They had no sooner sat down when servants came in bearing cakes and wine for them all.

Bruderic looked at the map and smiled. "You had made preparations for us, then?"

Hergard grinned. "As I said, I had hoped that you would come here, and thus I made preparations in case. And no matter what, I would need to make plans of my own, even if you had gone somewhere else."

Bruderic nodded. "My uncle and I discussed things on the way here. We want to send out messengers to as many Lords as possible. Including Lords we know to be loyal and those we think might be won from Nechtgang by the knowledge that the King lives."

"I have messengers standing by. All that is needed is to give them the word and say where they should go. Who do you plan to approach, and what do you plan to do?"

"What we plan to do is this: We will come to the capital on the day that Nechtgang has summoned the Lords to swear their oaths to him. We will gather as many as we are able before we go, and see if perhaps that might take the edge off those who are going without being too certain of themselves."

"There may be a risk in that, if Nechtgang has already gathered a sufficient force of his own. But it is quite true that there will be very many who will not wish to be the first nor the last to swear their oaths to him. Particularly if he is really to become King. Equally, Milord King, you must expect that there will be many who will not wish to be the first nor the last to take up your cause. Many will want to see which way the wind blows before they move."

"Yes indeed," said Bruderic, "And while they wait and watch, the wind may well come up and sweep them away altogether."

Carla felt a shiver of fear when Bruderic spoke thus. It reminded her too much of Lungand.

"Be that as it may, Highness, who do you wish to send word to?"

Bruderic began a list of names. Again, since Carla knew none of them, nor had she even heard rumours of few of them, she found this difficult to follow. She began to enjoy a tapestry on a wall. The tapestry which appeared to portray a young maiden sitting beside a stream, with a unicorn peeping shyly out from a bush behind her.

There was some argument about certain of the names on the list. So Carla continued to admire the skill which had gone into the work. The intricacy of the trees and bushes, the expression on the face of the unicorn, and the little rill in the stream running by the maiden's feet.

Eventually the planning was done. Messages were written up for the various people. Then a succession of men, lightly dressed and carrying only short swords, came in to take up their messages and be away. When the last of them had gone, Hergard said, "Now what?"

"Now we spend a while waiting. I presume that you have your own force ready to march at a moment's notice?"

Hergard grinned his huge grin. "Of course, Your Highness. And I have men out on all the roads to watch and warn in case Nechtgang should attempt to take this castle by a sudden storm. When do we march?"

"Tomorrow. We need a little time for our messengers to reach their destinations and for the Lords to set out. I know that many will be ready, even as you are. But we certainly must have the largest force we can manage, without waiting until the very last moment."

"True. And wish Nechtgang as little luck in gathering his forces as we have."

Hergard then turned to Wissagebreht. "Tell us, Wizard, these tales of what Gaistferu has done to the minds of men, what sort of magic is this?"

The Wizard scowled. "There are a number of tricks which may be used or misused. Just as a potion which eases pain may kill if administered in too large a dose, so other items in a magician's repertoire may be used wrongly. I have known Gaistferu for a long time, and have always known that his ambition and his ability could take him far, but for his fear of failure. Somewhere in the past week he has managed to overcome that fear. Having done so, he becomes able to do practically anything which would further his ambition."

"Do you hint that he may even displace Nechtgang?" inquired the Chamberlain.

"Possibly, but I doubt it. His wisest course, and I am sure he sees that as well as I, is to stand behind Nechtgang. Acting the loyal servant, but pressing his master into whatever action he thinks appropriate."

"Do we need to fear spells cast at a distance?"

"Probably not. I have sufficient strength to protect against such, and he surely knows that. What magic is likely to be used will be short-range spells. Apparitions conjured up at a particular time and place to influence the outcome of a single battle. Or perhaps spells used to aid in the taking of a particularly important castle. Most of the work will still go to the swords of the warriors."

Hergard was nodding his huge head as the Wizard spoke. "That relieves me. Swords and warriors I can fight, but I fear magic."

Carla could not help but remember the battle at Dumberlin's forge, and smile a bit.

Fresh clothing was delivered to them for the evening's meal. But despite the entertainments and the diversions of the night, the land was still on the edge of a war. As a result, there was a sombre undercurrent to it all.

Afterward, as they were on their way to their beds, Wissagebreht took an opportunity to speak to Carla. "We will be marching tomorrow. You may stay here in the castle."

He said it as though he were giving her a choice, but stating which choice he thought she should make. She thought it over for only a moment, then said, "No, I think I would rather come with you."

His eyebrows rose.

"I know practically no one here, and would much rather be with you."

"It may be dangerous."

She grinned openly at that. "So was Dumberlin's forge, but I was there."

He nodded, smiling. "The difference is that I brought you to the Caverns of the Dwarves willy-nilly. This time I am offering you a choice."

"And I choose to come along."

"So be it. I fear that they will not allow you to take part in any battles, though."

In the morning, Carla found that the servants had not brought back her travelling clothes. She dressed in the gown that had been lent to her for last evening, then went to look for someone to help her. Stepping into the corridor, she looked around to see where she was. There was nobody in sight. She went to Wissagebreht's room; the Wizard was already up and dressed, and looked at her when she came in.

"I know," she said, "I am not dressed for travelling, but the servants have not brought back my clothes."

"Ah," he said. "I don't suppose anyone realized that you would be travelling with us. Well, let us see what can be done."

He went to the door, and it happened that there was a young man, a page, passing by carrying a folded red cloak. "Young man," said Wissagebreht.

The boy turned to look at him.

"My ward here needs clothing more suitable for travelling. Could you find out what happened to the things she was wearing yesterday?"

"I will ask, sir." The boy looked up at Wissagebreht, gulped, and hurried off.

Carla looked after him. "Why is he so afraid of you?"

The Wizard grinned, with a bit of embarrassment in the grin. "He doesn't know me as well as you do, and is probably afraid that if he doesn't do what I want, I'll turn him into a toad. That is one of the unfortunate things about having power; it tends to set you apart from other people. So many of them fear that you could and would use your power for such petty purposes."

"And yet some do use their power for such petty purposes."

The Wizard nodded. "Some do. And that is another reason to fear Nechtgang and Gaistferu as rulers. They are too much interested in their own desires. Bruderic at least feels some responsibility for the welfare of his people."

They stood there for a while, talking about unimportant things. Then suddenly another page came hurrying up. "Milord Wissagebreht, his Highness asks if you are going to join them."

"Certainly. However, there is a difficulty. My ward here needs clothing more suitable for travelling."

The page looked at them, then gulped, his eyes widening. "Certainly, Milord! I will see to it immediately."

"No need. We have already sent off another lad to do that."

"But I will at least go see that it is being taken care of." He hurried off.

Wissagebreht shook his head. "That young man is frightened of me, and also frightened of what might happen when he goes back to tell the King what I have said."

It was not too much later that a young dark-haired servant-girl, very much flustered, came running up with a bundle of clothing in her hands. "You wanted travelling clothing, Milady?"

"Yes, I do."

"I have brought you a dress, and some riding boots."

Carla looked at the bundle in the girl's arms. "Those are not my clothes. They are not the things I was wearing yesterday."

The girl nearly broke down crying. "Oh, Milady, it was all a dreadful mistake! The clothes you were wearing were so old and worn that someone thought they were of no further use to anyone, and sent them out to be burned! No one knew that they belonged to you, or that—“

Carla put a hand on the girl's arm and quieted her. "No, no, these will be fine. Thank you."

Carla reached out to take the clothing out of the girl's hands, but she pulled away. "Oh, no, Milady, let me carry them to your room!"

She sounded a little scandalized that Carla would even think to carry her own things. Carla looked at Wissagebreht helplessly, but he was only smiling. She shrugged slightly and followed the girl to her room.

Chapter 9

ATTACK ON THE CAPITAL

By the time Carla had gotten into her clothing and hurried down to the courtyard, everyone else was ready and anxious to go. She barely had time to take note of the fact that what she was presently wearing was still far beyond the kind of dress she was used to.

The courtyard was full of men in armour and bright surcoats, mounted on tall, chestnut horses. For a moment, she did not recognize Bruderic or Lungand among them. But just as she was mounting the horse being held for her by a servant, the man next to her said, "So you are coming with us?" and she recognized the voice of the King.

"Yes," she said, simply.

His grin shone from under the helmet. "After having guarded Dumberlin's forge for a night, I will not warn you about the danger, but I hope you will be safe. And I am glad to have you along."

She wasn't quite sure what to say. But she gave Bruderic a close look and saw that under the carefree outside, he was burdened with sadness. She smiled. "But of course I had to come along," she said. "We have been together for too long for me not to want to see first-hand how things turn out."

She knew how foolish that sounded even as she said it, but it seemed to please Bruderic.

Outside the castle were rows of other men, mostly afoot. They were armed with swords, spears, and shields, all wearing bright coloured surcoats. As the mounted party rode out of the castle, these people began to march along behind them.

After they had gone a little way, Carla said, "We seem to have a large army with us."

Bruderic laughed, not unkindly. "Not really. All we have with us at the moment are Hergard's men. We will have more joining us on the way."

"Do soldiers always go so brightly dressed?"

"Yes, and for a good reason. Battles always begin with armies lined up in neat rows. But within minutes of the battle's beginning, those rows are bent and twisted. There is so much dust in the air that you can barely see the man in front of you. And when you see him, you may try to strike at him unless he's wearing the right colours and shouting the right shout. Despite that, many men are killed by their own fellows in the confusion."

As Bruderic had predicted, on their way, they were joined by several bands of men. Many as large as the band they were with. Carla and Wissagebreht were introduced to each of the Lords. Though Carla found herself mostly unable to keep them straight in her mind. She eventually hit upon the thought of remembering each one by the device on his shield and pennon, which helped very much.

One of the bands, numbering no more than twenty-five, was led by a man who was no more than two years older then Bruderic. He was slender, dark, handsome, and treated Carla with great politeness. His name was Gadmot, and he had recently come into the inheritance of his father's lands and title.

He first flattered Carla excessively. But when he saw that she was repelled by that he made his language a little less extreme. He could be very entertaining. He had a way of telling humourous anecdotes about everyone in such a manner that even the subject of the story would laugh. Nor did he spare himself in this regard, and some of his more amusing stories were of his own discomfiture.

Carla had been given a dark green cloak for warmth. She soon discovered that if she donned this cloak and stood still, remembering Wissagebreht's lessons on not being seen, people would pay no attention to her. In this way, she could overhear all the plans they were making.

This soon brought home to her the fact that they were in a situation little short of desperate. Nechtgang and Gaistferu had gathered a number of Lords to their cause by promising them rewards. More lands, more power within the Kingdom, and so on. Others had joined them out of fear. Because at the time Nechtgang set himself up Bruderic was missing, and they did not know when or if he would return.

There were many who were on the King's side. But some of these did not dare move just now, being so close under the eye of the usurper. Most accounts said that the King would have more troops when he arrived at the city. But that Nechtgang would have easily enough troops to defend the walls and hold the city. This by itself would convince many of his strength, and bring some waverers to his side. If, on the other hand, the King could take the city, he would attract many of those same waverers and thus be able to defeat Nechtgang.

And the King could not wait long. For there were a number of Lords in the outer territories gathering their forces on behalf of Nechtgang. Once those forces were gathered, unless the King had demonstrated his own strength, his army would be outnumbered. Then, if it came to a battle, they would be defeated.

Carla, seeing Bruderic more and more weighed down with all these problems, tried to spend a little time with him and cheer him up. Unfortunately, it seemed that every time they began to talk, someone needed to speak to the King about something. Whether it was authorization to forage for food in a particular neighbourhood. or be it authorization to requisition horses, arms. Or armour on promise of future payment, or a host of other problems. There were even certain of the Lords hinting that they would be even more loyal and willing to help the King if he could make a promise to better their circumstances when the war was over.

"After all," said one of these, "there will be a number of traitors to be gotten rid of, and someone must be given their lands."

In such cases the King made a promise that he would do his best to see that no man who remained loyal to him would suffer loss by that loyalty. This was not so strong a promise as was usually desired, but most of them feared to press the King too hard in such a matter.

For two days they marched towards the capital. It was long and arduous, Carla was surprised by how much more slowly they moved now that there were so many more people with them. But the army had to stop often in order to rest animals, eat and to ensure that other sections caught up who may have lagged behind. Two nights they spent in tents. Again, Carla noted that the set up of the camp took much longer than when it was just the four of them. Around which the campfires of their growing army flamed and smoked. Soldiers gathered, talking, eating, laughing, and speaking of everything except the of battle which must come.

On the third day, they came to the ridge outside the capital and camped again, just out of sight of the city. Most of the Lords went with the King to view the situation in order to make plans. While Carla, by simply riding along as though she belonged there, accompanied them.

Even from this distance they could see that the tall, stony walls were manned. Therefore, would be little or no possibility of their army approaching the city unseen. Save perhaps at night. Even that would require them to move much more quietly than any of the Lords expected to be possible.

Small parties of men on horseback were approaching the city by all the visible roads into the city. Most of these carried pennons declaring which Lord was coming. Carla saw Lungand's face go grim as he looked at them.

Bruderic spoke. "One of the first things to do is to send parties out to watch the roads. Inform the Lords going in that the King wishes to speak to them."

Hergard, who appeared to have taken the place of Commander along with Lungand, nodded. "True. But you will notice, Milord King, that few of the Lords are bringing more than ten men-at-arms with them. This means that the Usurper will have sworn support from many Lords, but few troops with which to fight us. if we can bring him to battle before those Lords can send for their armies, we have an advantage."

"Yes. And the fewer Lords he has to call on, the better for us. From the looks of it, Nechtgang has sufficient troops to hold the city against us. If we attempt to storm the walls. The chances are that we will lose so many in the attack that even if we get over the walls, we will be unable to do much else.

"So. We will have to send out word to every Lord within a few days' march to join us here. If we can build up our force quickly enough, we may be able to take the city. If we do not, then we are going to have to stay outside, building up support, and eventually putting the city under siege. And that will prove who is the more popular, myself or Nechtgang."

"And Nechtgang will be promising to his various Lords all the properties of those who are on our side. We cannot wait too long, Milord." Said Lungand.

"No. But there is little more we can do here. Hergard, please assign a few men to keep watch from here in case anything happens. Such as Nechtgang sending his army out against us.", Said Bruderic.

That was done, and the rest of them went back to where the bulk of the host was still in the process of setting up a camp. The King and the Lords began to talk about all the various methods which might be used to get into the city, most of them risky at best, and fatal if anything went wrong. After a bit of this, Carla drifted away, watching all the barely organized disorder in the camp around her.

"One wonders, doesn't one, whether half of them really know what they're doing," said a soft voice at her shoulder.

She jumped a little, then turned. Gadmot was smiling at her. She smiled back. “Shouldn’t you be over with the others, making plans?"

He shrugged his elegant and dismissive shrug. "I come with a scarce twenty-five men at my back. With the possibility of perhaps that many again if I call on every male who is able to walk. And bring them to war armed with pitchforks. And I am a mere boy, inexperienced in war. So they would prefer not to hear from me at all."

He looked over his shoulder at the Lords all discussing and expostulating. "No, all I should get from them if I pressed myself into their counsels would be dreadful frowns from all. And too many frowns from too many old men could easily turn me into just as disagreeable a person as they are."

Again he shrugged. "So rather than that, I come to talk to one other person who is out of the counsels."

He asked how she had come to be with the King, and she explained that they had been on a quest together. He knew that they had been on a quest, and with careful questions he drew out of her what the quest had entailed. As he learned more and more, he began looking at her with almost awe.

"Well," he said at last, "you have had more experience in battle than I! Perhaps you ought to be part of the counsel."

Carla laughed. "They are deciding how to use huge armies; my battles have only been small, involving the four of us. I wouldn't know how to use an army if anyone asked me, and to tell the truth, I'd rather not."

Their conversation went on into other less serious fields then. She was a little angry when Bruderic came and interrupted them.

Bruderic seemed upset himself, and she couldn't quite be sure what it was. She felt perhaps it was merely the same thing that had been bothering him since they had first found out about the rebellion. So she did what she could to talk to him, though it was not the same as talking to Gadmot.

The only plan they had been able to come up with was to wait for more men to join them before trying an attack. For they all knew, more men would also be joining Nechtgang. Therefore they could not wait too long before taking some sort of action.

About the middle of the next day, a young man came into the camp. He had been wearing a dark brown cloak which made him look much like a common man. But at the camp, he threw off the cloak to reveal his surcoat which showed an arm brandishing a mace. The guards brought him to the King almost immediately.

He bowed and said, "Milord King, I am Bridwic the son of Hargrad, and I am come to offer our services to you."

Bruderic looked skeptical. "In what way do you plan to serve me? Do you have soldiers nearby to join us?"

"Even better, Milord King, we have a plan to aid you to get into the city."

Bruderic raised his eyebrows. "Indeed?"

"Indeed. You see, Milord King. My father and I were both inside the city when Nechtgang made his declaration, and it was not possible to escape. Also, the Wizard Gaistferu was watching and listening to all, seeing who was loyal and who was not. We dared not do other than what we did, to swear allegiance to Nechtgang, but look for our opportunity.

"What my father has planned is that this afternoon he will open the gates to the city. And hold them with his men long enough for you to bring a force in."

Bruderic smiled. "It seems to be possible. I suppose he has made his whole plan known to you?"

"Of course, since that is the only way it would work, Milord King. All he asks is that you yourself come down to the gate so that he will know that you are accepting his terms and his plan. You could bring a small band of your people. About ten or so, and disguise yourselves as peasants in order to come through the gates. When he sees you there, he will give orders to his men. Who will be waiting thereabouts, and they will take control of the gates. Holding them open until your main force can arrive."

Lungand shook his head. "The plan is good, but we cannot risk sending the King himself down there."

The young man shrugged. "My father will not act unless he sees the King himself. You understand, there are so many people declaring their loyalty or changing their loyalty. That anyone could claim to be from the King. In such a case, my father would be caught in treason to Nechtgang and executed. The King himself must come. And to prove that he has no treachery in mind, my father is offering me as a hostage for your safety."

"So." Bruderic frowned. "I must discuss this with my Lords and advisers. Will you please wait?"

The young man nodded and the army held council on what was to be done. The general attitude toward this plan was negative. It was risky to place the King thus at the head of the small group which would be at the mercy of whoever would be waiting at the gates. It would take a long while for the main force to come up, and during that time the King might well be killed or captured.

The King shook his head. "I think treachery is unlikely; after all, we have his son here. And as for me being alone there. Well, I shall be at risk in any battle we fight, unless I sit back and let my people do all the fighting on my behalf. If we pick the men carefully who will come with me, then even if there is treason. It is possible that we can hold the gates open until the rest arrive."

Lungand shook his head. "Too many risks, Milord King."

"And what of the victory if we do actually take the city from Nechtgang? If we take him there, we will end the rebellion in one stroke. If he escapes, we have the capital, and we have proven him less capable than he claims. We must try."

Lungand shook his head. "Milord, even if we do come in through this gate, Nechtgang has an advantage. He will know we are coming. For the matter will not be hidden from his loyal troops, and we will have to fight for every street and alley. And being able to bring our troops in only at one point, we will have a definite disadvantage."

Bruderic frowned in thought for a moment, then he spoke. "So while our first attack comes in through the gate, we send a rapid storming party to another point on the wall. Even if they do not succeed in coming over the wall, they will force Nechtgang to divide his own forces."

"But you will still be there at the front, and if it is treachery, then they need only let you in and slam the gate behind you. Whatever force we send in then would be fruitless."

Wissagebreht spoke up then. "I have some thoughts on that. It might be possible to arrange things so that the gates could not be closed easily."

Carla sat her horse on the ridge overlooking the city, in the midst of the vanguard of Hergard's army. Hergard himself, fully armed, sat beside her. He had his helmet off, slung at his saddle, and his red hair seemed more wild and shaggy than ever. There was a grim sadness in his eyes, as though he could see the sorrow this day would bring, but could see no way to avoid it.

Down the road in front of them was a party of ten men dressed as peasants. They carried sacks over their shoulders. They appeared to be carrying their produce to market. That was the King and Lungand and the few men in their party.

A little ahead of them were three oxcarts. These were huge lumbering vehicles with two huge wheels each. Wheels built by strapping a set of heavy planks together, then cutting wheels out of them. They made a dreadful squealing, though that was barely audible from this distance. On the oxcarts were Wissagebreht and ten others. A small addition to the force with the King personally.

Way down below the city stood. All seemed calm and normal, though there were more men on the walls than would be there in peacetime. Small bands of nobles with a few men were still on the roads toward the city. No few of these had been intercepted by the King's men and sent on up to the King's camp. But some still felt that their best interest lay with Nechtgang and Gaistferu.

Carla looked around. The first group of soldiers were about fifty mounted men who would ride hell-for-leather down the road to get to the gates. Once there, they would reinforce that dreadfully small band as the King reached the gates. In that group was Gadmot. As her eyes fell on him he smiled at her.

Gadmot had told Carla earlier that he begged to go in this group, “For some reason," he said with his little grin and shrug, "They thought I could as well die in this way as any other."

Despite that bravado, his face was a little pale, and his smile was a little forced. His hand held a lance which he was alternately squeezing and loosening, as though he sought a better grip. But this was more likely a case of nerves.

That force was headed by another leader, a grizzled soldier by the name of Grinhald, who sat still with little expression. Some of the men were mounted. Others were still afoot. Others were loosening up muscles, checking the harness of their horse, taking a last drink of water or wine, or just talking to their neighbours.

The men on foot were overtaking the oxcarts now. They were passing the odd word between them as would be expected of such groups on the way to town.

Carla looked at Hergard. He was looking down at the city in such a way that it looked as though he were willing things to happen. She moved nervously in the saddle, and the horse responded by shuffling its own feet. Hergard looked over at her, then smiled. "Patience, young Carla. It is barely begun."

She forced herself to return his smile, but she could not help but feel frightened of what was to come. Even if this was no trap and Hargrad was waiting to hold the gate for them. There would still follow a tremendous battle before the city was taken and Bruderic would be in that battle.

"Milord Hergard, surely this will be no trap, will it? After all, Bridwic is here as hostage, and his father will surely not risk his life, will he?"

Hergard tried to smile reassuringly, but failed. "Probably not, but there is a chance. After all, if this is treachery, they are acting with the knowledge of Nechtgang. If the King is taken or killed, our cause will fall apart immediately. And who would want to be the person to kill Bridwic, knowing that his father will have great influence with the Usurper?"

"Then why does the King risk himself in this way?"

She had heard the answers, she knew them well, but she had to talk about something.

"Because there is a chance that this is no treachery. However, even if it is, there is still a possibility that we can turn it against them. And if we can do that, then we will have struck a strong blow against the Usurper. Perhaps we might even make it impossible for him to fight much longer."

They were silent then, watching the two groups slowly travel the road to the city. They were wearing chainmail and surcoats under the peasant garb. Which would likely fool anyone who did not look too closely at them. Of course, all it would need would be one flash of metal or one glimpse of colour which ought not to be on a peasant, and they would be betrayed.

At last, at long last, they had reached the gate. Grinhald half-turned his head and said, "All right, you lot. Get mounted up; it's time."

Hergard moved his horse a little out of the way, and Carla did the same. There was movement down at the gates now, metal flashing in the sun. “For King Bruderic!" shouted Grinhald, and was away. Behind him his small band put spurs to their horses and followed.

No sooner were they out of the way when Hergard clapped on his helm and called to his Captains, "Forward, for King Bruderic!"

They advanced, marching steadily downward toward the city. Leaving Carla with the three men-at-arms who had been told off to guard her. They were not rushing as Grinhald's men, for they were expecting to come in through the gate and fight their way through the streets. Grinhald and his men were merely to provide immediate protection for the King.

There was confusion down at the gates now. There were flashes of colour as Bruderic's men tore off the peasant garb to make themselves known. Carla could see the oxcarts too. Wissagebreht and the other drivers had taken them as close to the gates as possible. They jumped down, cut the traces, and cut the tongues of the carts. Then they smashed the wooden bands that held the wheels together. It would now be something of a job to move the carts, and that must be done before the gates could be closed. Grinhald's men ought to be there before that could be done.

She strained her eyes to pick out Bruderic in that struggling knot of men in the gate. But she knew that at this distance it would be impossible. They seemed to be being pushed back, back through the gateway. No, wait! They were holding! Then slowly they were being pushed back, and men in Nechtgang's colours were heaving at the carts.

Suddenly Grinhald's men came crashing in. Then a little later she could faintly hear the shouts from below. Now they were back within the gates, moving inward. They were out of her sight now. Had they moved too far and too fast? If the gates were shut behind them now—!

At that moment some people in Bruderic's colours took up positions at the gates to prevent just that. Carla could see the bodies lying in the gateway. People in both Bruderic's and Nechtgang's colours. She wondered again if Bruderic were safe. But surely if he were not, they would have already fallen back?

Then the vanguard of Hergard's men were in the gateway, and now the shouting redoubled. At this distance it was not possible to make out the individual shouts, but the noise swelled. There was a cloud of dust in the gateway now, and Carla remembered Bruderic's explanation of the surcoats.

The advance of Hergard's men was suddenly halted. About half the column still protruding out of the gate like a strange tail. Out of that column came several small parties, running to the walls. Some of them set ladders against the walls and began to climb. While others shot arrows up to keep defenders back.

Some of the ladders were toppled. But in two places the attackers managed to reach the top. Then there was a fight around the heads of the ladders as more men mounted them. Now the wall was taken for several hundred feet on each side of the gate. More ladders were being brought up as more and more of the column went up over the wall.

Shortly after that the column began to move again. A little later the last of them had disappeared inside, leaving a few men to hold the gates.

A moment later Carla saw another forest of spears moving across the plain. That was the second force. Which was to assault the walls on the far side of the city and draw off more of Nechtgang's soldiers. After a little, even that column was out of sight beyond the city, and there was nothing left to watch.

Carla looked around her. There were a few men too badly lame or too sick to join the attack, and a few of the women who followed the army standing and watching. There was also a small contingent of men-at-arms, under the command of a certain Terbold, who had been ordered to watch the camp. There was nothing to watch any longer, but eventually the battle would be won or lost. Then it would be time to bandage wounds and count the dead.

This suddenly brought to mind the fact that there were few medicines with the army. They would need potions to ease pain. She called some of the women over and they came, cautiously, for she was clearly a woman of rank. As such, she was potentially dangerous to them. Carla remembered her own feelings about nobles when Bruderic and Lungand had first ridden into her life and she smiled slightly.

In a few minutes Carla had most of the women off looking for the proper plants. While she herself was giving orders as to how they should be prepared. All of this kept her busy enough so that she seldom had a moment to give thought to what might be happening as Bruderic and his men fought their way through the twisting streets of the city.

They had just gotten the mixture into its final stages where it had to cool off. When Carla heard a sound of rapid hooves coming into the camp. She looked up to see a sweaty, dirty rider on a dusty tired looking steed coming up to Terbold. She walked over, wiping sweat from her brow, in time to hear the message.

"The city is taken, Nechtgang and his people have fled. The King commands you to bring the camp to the city. He further commands that there is to be no plundering, on pain of death."

There was a bit of muttering from the people around at that last order. Long tradition held that the people who accompanied the army had the right to plunder enemy camps or captured cities. This was of course in exchange for their help with the camp and their care for the sick and the wounded. In this case, however, the city was the capital city. The city of the King, and there had been little likelihood that he would allow it to be looted.

Terbold turned and began to give orders to the camp guards to get everything ready to be moved down to the city. He also passed along the order that there was to be no looting. That done, he looked around again. Seeing Carla, he approached her. Dragging his left leg which kept him out of active fighting, Terbold asked, "Are you sure you'll want to come with us, Milady? After the battle, it will not be a pleasant sight."

Her status had changed very much, it seemed. She still could not get used to people being so polite to her.

"I will go down to the city, Terbold. I have seen a battle before. Please make sure that this gets delivered as well," She waved toward the cooling potion, "I imagine that Wissagebreht will be caring for the wounded, and if so, he will appreciate having it."

The carts and wagons creaked and jounced down toward the city. Carla, with barely restrained impatience, walked her horse among the guards. Terbold would have been quite upset had she attempted to gallop down alone. He would then almost certainly have sent men to bring her back. This was another side of the politeness she was being shown. She was a friend of the King. Therefore, anybody who carelessly allowed her to go into danger felt sure that they faced the wrath of the King.

A camp was set up outside the gates of the castle. Again, there was a long period of waiting. Around the gates were several soldiers in the colours of both sides. Most of them were lying still and lifeless, but one or two moaned slightly. Terbold sent some of the people of the camp to look to them and see if anything could be done, but mostly they waited.

Soldiers came out to the camp occasionally on ill-defined errands. Carla tried to gather information as the soldier came in. Unfortunately she was only able to get little tidbits such as was that it had been a dreadful battle, that the King and Hergard were safe, that Grinhald had taken several wounds but was still on his feet, and that Lungand was as ill-tempered as ever.

Wissagebreht came out finally, looking around a bit grimly, then came over to the camp. Carla went forward to meet him, explaining how she had had the people brewing the potion while the battle was going on. He nodded, smiling slightly. "Good, good, I knew I could rely on you to use your head. Now, we need some people to come in and care for the wounded."

"I want to come in too."

He looked at her in sudden surprise, but said only, "Then come along."

"Would you speak to my guards? They seem afraid that I would either get hurt or get too upset at the sight of the aftermath of battle."

He nodded. "I will talk to them. But now I have to speak to Terbold."

The path they took through the city was essentially the same one on which most of the fighting had been done. It was marked with bodies in bright-coloured surcoats, men who had been killed or wounded in the attack. By now parties of soldiers were collecting the wounded. But they were collecting at the far end of the path and working toward the gates.

She could tell the places where the defenders had made their stands, for these were the places where the soldiers lay thickest. The King's and the Usurper's, mixed in their rows.

They came at last to the palace, where the attack had culminated. In fact, by the time the fighting had reached that point Nechtgang was already fleeing, leaving only a few of his troops to delay the King's forces. All that had been left afterwards, was a pursuit. A running fight as that rearguard sought to make its way out of the city before being surrounded and overwhelmed.

They finally reached the palace steps where Bruderic was standing. He was giving orders to various officers regarding disposition of prisoners, defence of the walls, and a host of other such details. Carla dismounted and waited patiently. Bruderic was mostly setting capable men in charge of various things. In the end, many men in the crowd who had a question for the King found before they reached him that it was not the King they had to see, but someone else.

Finally the last of the soldiers turned away, and Bruderic was able to look at Carla.

"Welcome to my city and my palace, Carla," he said.

He was smiling, but Carla could see the strain on his mouth, the weariness in his eyes, and the grey colour of his skin. He had washed his hands and face, but his surcoat was slashed and stained. There was no doubt that he had been in battle.

Carla tried to think of something to say, but all she could do was smile. It was Bruderic himself who broke the silence. "Well, this battle has been won, but there will be others to fight, and I must have some rest and some food. Will you join me?"

"Yes, thank you. Where is Lungand?", asked Carla.

Bruderic smiled again. "Ah, he has already taken charge of seeing that there are servants in the palace and that they are doing their duty. Wissagebreht, will you join us?"

"Very shortly, Bruderic. There are still a few things to be done," said Wissagebreht.

Bruderic hesitated. "What more?"

Wissagebreht smiled. "No, nothing that requires the presence of the King, only that I wish to see to the comfort of the wounded."

The King smiled slightly, "If my uncle heard you speak thus, he would teach you better. 'The King goes into battle first, and is the last to find rest afterward.'

"But I will go see if there is a small bite of food to be had in the kitchen. Then see if there is a clean surcoat to be found, then finally, I will come visit the wounded myself. Thank you, Wissagebreht, for reminding me of my duty, even though it robs me of a meal," but he smiled as he spoke.

Carla wanted to go with him, but she was also thinking of what she had seen on the way to the palace. "I will go with Wissagebreht, Bruderic, and perhaps see you later. I'm glad to see you well."

"Well? Ah, I suppose that I am well enough in body, only one or two scratches. But I am not really well. I have seen men today, Carla. Men who were once my playmates screaming at me across shield-rims. And now that the battle is over I cannot say whether or not I hope that they are safe."

His body sagged for a moment, then he drew himself up. "Ah well, there will be much to be put right once Nechtgang has been taken care of." He turned and walked up the palace steps.

Chapter 10

THE FINAL BATTLE

The wounded had been gathered. At first they were placed in several large storehouses. Then when the storehouses were full, tents were erected around them. Wissagebreht went through the encampments, taking Carla with him. She started at one side and he at the other. They examined each wound, giving instructions as to how it should be treated. In several cases, Carla was not certain as to how to treat a particular wound. She would then leave that one for the Wizard to look at personally.

The people who cared for the wounded were at first wary of Carla, knowing her to be a friend of the King. But as she went on, they saw that she knew what she was about, and they became easier with her.

As for Carla herself, living with an herb-wizard she had come to see all manner or hurts and illnesses. But now she was faced with large numbers of injuries. After the first three she wanted to leave, to go somewhere else where she wouldn't need to look at injured men. But she remembered that it had been her decision to come into the city. Now that she was here, she had best do something to make herself useful.

In the third of the storehouses of wounded, about quarter of the way through, she found herself looking at Gadmot. He had taken a spear through the thigh, and had lost quite a lot of blood, so that he was extremely pale. He was unconscious, but the healers had done what they could for him, and it seemed likely that he would live. She was just leaving him to go on to the next man when he opened his eyes briefly, looked up at her, smiled, and went to sleep again.

By the time they had gone through that house, she was so tired that she was practically falling asleep on her feet. Wissagebreht looked at her and said, "Go find a bed to crawl into, Carla. You can do little more good in this condition."

All she could do was to stare at him blankly, so he called a servant to take her and find her a place to sleep in the palace. She couldn't remember anything more of the night after that.

Morning came and Carla, after getting dressed and finding a bite to eat, went out to see if Gadmot was still alive. He was alive, awake, and very weak. He smiled as she approached.

"Good morning to you, Carla."

"Good morning to you, Gadmot. I won't ask how you feel."

His smile grew a little broader. "I managed to stay with the King almost to the step of the palace. Then suddenly there was a blow on my leg and I was lying on the ground with a spear through my thigh. I don't remember anything after that, save that I thought I woke once to see you standing over me. But I suppose that was only a dream."

"No, no dream. I spent some time helping to treat the wounded, and you woke for just a moment while I was here."

"Ah." He seemed to be trying to find something more to say, but suddenly his eyes shifted to a point just over her shoulder. She turned to see Lungand standing there.

Lungand smiled at Gadmot. "I'm pleased to see you so well, young man. The King will certainly come to express his own gratitude. But I wished to see to it that you know that your deeds have not gone unrecognized."

"Thank you, Milord Chamberlain."

"Oh no, it is I that thank you. Be certain that you will not be forgotten, Gadmot."

The Chamberlain turned and walked away.

Carla looked again at Gadmot. "So you are a hero, too?"

He tried to shrug, a difficult feat while lying down. "All I did was try to keep within sight of the King, and hit anyone who wasn't wearing the right colour. I think I may have killed a couple of dogs or cats who didn't get out of the way in time."

She chuckled. "I can imagine. But if I stand here talking to you for any time, Wissagebreht will come and shout at me to let you rest. So rest, now."

"You will come again?"

"Oh, I will come again from time to time."

As she turned away, one of the healers approached her a little diffidently. He was a short, stout man, dressed mostly in grey, with a grey beard and a ruff of grey hair surrounding a pink bald spot. He had seen her at work the previous day, and recognized her skill. At this moment there was a particular case he would like her to look at, to see if there was anything she could do for him.

She thought to suggest that he go find Wissagebreht. But no sooner did the thought come to her than she realized that the Wizard would himself be busy with the same sort of thing. And though she was nowhere near as expert as Wissagebreht, she had learned much from him. Perhaps there might be something she could offer.

There were several more cases which the healer asked her to look at. Despite that she was out again about noon when Hargrad came in, under a flag of truce. Bruderic met him on the palace steps, looking at him sternly, waiting for whatever Hargrad might say.

Hargrad dismounted and knelt in front of the King. "Milord King, I have come to beg for the life of my son."

"You sent your son as part of a trick to trap me, giving his life as a surety that there would be no treachery. Why should he not suffer the fate for which he offered himself?"

"Milord King, he is my only son! I have come to offer my own life in exchange for his, if need be."

The King considered that for a moment or two. "Is this perhaps a way of changing allegiances for you, having seen that Nechtgang is not so powerful as he had thought?"

"Milord, you will believe what you will. All I can say is what I have said; I come to save my son."

Bruderic nodded. "So be it. Your life and the life of your son are safe, at least for now. Yet you will have to pay for your treachery eventually. That price will be decided later, when we have more leisure. For the present, you and your son shall remain in custody here."

Hargrad rose, and there were unmistakable tears in his eyes, but he said simply, "Thank you, Milord King."

There were mutterings from the people assembled there, and Bruderic heard them. He looked out at the crowd. "I see this displeases many of you. Yes indeed, there are men who deserve punishment for their deeds. And punishment they will have. But if the Lords following Nechtgang see that they may have lenient treatment should they desert him, when the war begins to go against them. They may well change their allegiance again.

"But if they see that they die whether they fight or surrender, then will they not fight all the harder? And I think that none of us wish to encourage them to fight harder."

There were several smiles in the crowd at that. Though they were clearly not all happy, they were at least satisfied for the time being.

Bruderic remained in the capital for some time, gathering his forces. He also had scouts out to see just what Nechtgang was up to. They brought back word that Nechtgang was also gathering forces. Gaistferu the Wizard was with him. He was using his powers to frighten and cow both those who were unwilling to join him and those who were had become less willing to continue following him.

It was even said that Gaistferu had used his power to blast holes in the walls of certain castles whose Lords were unwilling to join the rebels.

This, of course, led some of Bruderic's Lords to demand that Wissagebreht do the same to the castles of those who supported Nechtgang. Wissagebreht heard the demands. Quietly stroking his beard, then said, "There is no doubt that I could do this, but the result could be disastrous. You see, we do not know the whereabouts of Nechtgang's forces. And Gaistferu has hidden them from any search by magical means and covered them with protection from any spells I might try.

"Each time he attacks a castle, he must either weaken or withdraw completely his spells of concealment and protection. And there is a risk that if I were ready at that precise moment, I might find the army and attack them.

"Gaistferu has an advantage; he knows where we are. If I withdraw or weaken my protection in order to attack a castle, he might well wreak havoc among us."

This did not quite satisfy Wyrgenhelm. "So we sit here waiting while he smashes our castles about our ears?"

Wissagebreht smiled gently. "Oh, I think not. A look at the map will show that the castles being attacked are those in certain strategic positions. Those which cover certain supply and trade routes. Gaistferu is quite well aware of the risk of weakening his protective spells in order to attack. So most of our castles need fear no magical attack."

"But if we cannot find Nechtgang's army, what is to hinder Gaistferu from doing as he wishes? You yourself said---"

"I myself said that their army was protected from my searching spells. We also have scouts and patrols out across the land. Along with the fact that every attack which they make, magical or not, gives us some hint as to where they are. When we have found them, by whatever means, then we are on more even terms."

Another week went by, with no more than continued patrols and scouting. Some patrols and scouts occasionally encountering enemy patrols or scouts. Little coloured markers were set on the map to mark where troops were known to be, both friendly and enemy. Out of all this a notion of Nechtgang's location began to show itself.

Both Bruderic and Lungand were a little more upset than they let on about the paucity of Lords coming to declare their loyalty for King Bruderic since the capital had been taken. It came to the point where the chamberlain sent messengers with hints, which were little less than thinly veiled summonses that they should appear before the King.

Wissagebreht was less concerned about that. "Most of them are still waiting to see who has the advantage. We did take the capital from Nechtgang, but he was able to withdraw with most of his force. And then there is the fear of Gaistferu. We have plenty of troops at present, and we will pick up a few more before the time comes to give battle."

By the end of that week Gadmot was up, hobbling along with an old spearshaft for a crutch. Carla divided her time between Gadmot and Bruderic.

Though Bruderic was too often busy with the business of preparing for the war. Carla also remained curious about the planning. Using the means she had already perfected, standing still in her green cloak, she was able to learn a great deal.

On the last day of the week, Bruderic's council was interrupted by the word that a party of upwards of twenty Dwarves were coming through the gate, driving four large wagons. They announced that they were making a delivery for the King. The King immediately adjourned the council in order to meet them.

Very shortly after they had gone out on the steps, the Dwarf-wagons rolled into the palace square. Vashchi himself rode beside the driver of the first wagon, looking very pleased with himself.

It was not uncommon for Dwarves to come to the city, but never in such numbers and such heavily-laden wagons. As a result a good number of the people were in the palace square when the wagons arrived, and more kept coming. The wagons rolled to a stop, and Vashchi hopped down, walked to the palace step, and bowed to the King.

"Milord King of Vorholm, as agreed, we bring the memorial you purchased. Where shall we set it up?"

Bruderic gave it a moment's thought, then said, "Here in this square, before these steps."

Vashchi bowed again, then turned and spoke a single word of command in Dwarvish. Twenty or more Dwarves jumped out of the wagons and all began moving at once. With so many moving around in such a space, it seemed inevitable that some should bump into each other. They never so much as brushed shoulders, going this way and that. It was as though that they were in some kind of complicated dance where every performer moved in concert with all the others.

They set up tripods, hooked up pulleys and winches, and set to work with a will. They set up a stone column twice the height of a man. On the top of which they set a tree, no more than a foot and a half tall. All of it worked gold, so intricately crafted that it looked as though it had grown naturally. On the tree were small fruit, in the form of small red jewels along the branches.

It was the kind of thing which could very easily have looked cheap and gaudy. But in this case each part balanced every other part so that the whole had a pleasing effect.

When they were done, Vashchi turned to Bruderic and said, "Well, Milord King of Vorholm? Does it please you?"

The King took his time answering. But when he did he said, "Vashchi, 'beautiful' is such an inappropriate word. But for this work, there is little else to say. The Dwarves are well renowned for their craftsmanship with metals."

Vashchi tried hard to keep a solemn face, but it was plain that he was pleased with the King's speech. "It was fairly bought and paid for, Milord King of Vorholm. Long may it stand."

"Long may it stand indeed," answered the King, his mind brought to the reason for the memorial. For a moment he stood in silence, then he spoke again. "Will you and your party accept our hospitality, as the four of us accepted your hospitality under the mountain?"

Vashchi hesitated only a moment, then answered, "Yes Milord, we will, and gladly."

At that moment there was a mutter of awe in the crowd around. one which seemed to spread from one particular place and sweep out around the circle. Into the palace square trotted a unicorn. Without looking more than once, Carla recognized him. “Quickfoot!” she said.

With only a slight hesitation in order to pick her out from all the others around, Yssarit trotted over to her, and bowed his head.

"Quickfoot," she said, "Why are you here?"

The familiar laughter was in his voice. "Why, just as the leaving of the unicorns was the sign of the beginning of evil times for Vorholm. So must the return of the unicorns be the sign of the end of those evil times."

"But the memorial is barely erected! You must have been in Vorholm for some time!"

"But the Elves have ways of knowing many things. They knew that barring some sort of strange mischance, the memorial would be delivered. And I have come at the express command of Queen Serenglas. To bring a message of goodwill to all in the land, and to bring special greetings to you, young Carla. And I see that you have come up in the world from the time when first I saw you."

"Yes, I suppose I have. And thank you for the message from the Queen."

The unicorn made a motion which was as near to a shrug as could be. "It was a message I was glad to bring. Now, however, I must say that I do not feel comfortable in the presence of so great a crowd. With your leave, I shall go. But perhaps we shall see each other on another day."

"I hope so. Farewell, Quickfoot."

"And farewell to you, young Carla."

The unicorn turned and trotted away, and the crowd parted for him. As he disappeared down the street, Carla was suddenly aware of the people crowded around the square and staring. They were staring at her, as though she was something strange and wonderful. She looked around, and saw that almost the only ones without similar expressions were Wissagebreht, who held a small secret smile, Lungand, with a look which was slightly less grim than usual, and Bruderic, who had a look that she could not quite interpret.

All those stares were like a weight on her shoulders. So much so that she was on the point of running away and hiding alone somewhere inside the palace. But suddenly Wissagebreht spoke. "Look to the sky, people of Vorholm!"

Everyone looked up and saw that the sky, which had been blue save for a few ragged wisps of cloud here and there, was changing. Those ragged wisps of cloud were rushing together, becoming larger and darker. Until there was not a bit of blue to be seen. Then the rain began to fall, softly and steadily. A rain which was clearly unlike any of the small showers which Vorholm had seen in the past five years.

It was a rain which any of the weather-wise old folk in the crowd knew would last for at least a day, perhaps several days. And as it began to come home to them what had happened, the people began to rejoice. Bruderic and his council, after standing in the rain for a little while, retreated up the steps to the shelter of the porch. Down below, the people of the city were singing and dancing as the rain fell, for the curse had been lifted from the land.

***   ***

Two weeks later, King Bruderic's host was arrayed on one side of a valley, looking at the host of Nechtgang on the other side. The armies were so near equal in size that it was clear to all that the battle would be a near thing. Carla was with them as well, having stood up not only to Bruderic but to Wissagebreht as well when they suggested that she might want to stay in the capital.

"By no means!" she had said. "If you are going, I shall go too. And you know that I shall not go simply as another burden to you. For even you, Wissagebreht, must admit that I can be of some use to you in caring for the wounded. I am coming with you, and that is that."

Wissagebreht, recognizing her determination, had merely shrugged. Bruderic, looking to the Wizard for support and finding none, had also been forced to let the issue drop. She sat her horse on the hillside behind the main army, guarded again by three men-at-arms. Wissagebreht was on a hillside behind and slightly to the right of the army, watching for Gaistferu.

In each army the foot-soldiers were in the front line, pikemen and swordsmen, with bowmen just behind them. Behind these were the horse, divided into several groups, each under a particular leader.

In the King's army, each leader waited for Bruderic's orders. Bruderic had explained his thinking in the council the previous night. "With our forces as they are, every movement must be carefully judged. Our horsemen will be sent in to any place where it seems possible that they might break through the enemy line or in any place where the enemy threatens to break through ours."

There had been some questions. Some protests about being too cautious. That it would be better to simply charge with all the troops and overrun Nechtgang before he could get ready. Bruderic, with support from Lungand and Hergard, overrode all these objections. And so it was that the two armies met the next day regarding each other warily from opposite sides of the valley.

A solitary black figure appeared suddenly on a hilltop behind Nechtgang's forces. A mutter immediately went up from the King's army, almost as immediately hushed by the under-officers in the ranks. Gaistferu, for it was indeed he, stretched up his left hand bearing his staff toward the sky, and pointed a finger at Wissagebreht.

A ball of light was suddenly at his fingertip, then rushing swiftly across the valley with a sort of screaming hiss. Well before it reached him, however, Wissagebreht held up a palm. The ball of light began to slow and fade, until it dissipated completely.

At that moment a bolt of lightning struck down at Wissagebreht, but he stood unharmed. Wissagebreht gestured himself, and sent a ball of flame towards Gaistferu. Gaistferu threw up an invisible barrier and halted it with ease. The magical battle was on in dead earnest. Balls of flame, of blue, orange, yellow, and various other colours screamed through the air. Wissagebreht and Gaistferu both glancing the missiles of with unseen armour. Bolts of lightning streaked down from the sky, leaving smouldering ground in their wake. Beams of diverse hues flashed through the air from pointed fingers.

At first each Wizard was able to dissipate harmlessly any spells used by the other. But they eventually, became too weary to do more than deflect them. The ground around each of them became burned and blackened, with great gouges hacked in it. Smoke and dust surrounded them.

It was impossible to make out Gaistferu on his hilltop. But when Carla looked at Wissagebreht, she could see that he was leaning heavily on his staff. She was suddenly frightened that this Wizard, the man who had raised her, who had always seemed able to accomplish anything, had met his match.

At that very moment Wissagebreht seemed to gather himself up, stand erect, and speak one word. There was a sudden bright flash of flame from the hill where Gaistferu stood, a flame which temporarily blinded the eyes of those watching. When they could see again, they saw that the blast appeared to have cleared most of the smoke and dust from the air for the moment. But Gaistferu was nowhere to be seen.

Carla looked back at Wissagebreht and saw him strive to steady himself with his staff, then slowly collapse to the ground. She turned her horse and galloped up the hill, letting her guards follow her as they would. She leaped down beside him, and saw that the Wizard was unconscious, breathing very lightly, much as he had been after leaving Lothbosc.

That thought told her what she should do next. She turned to one of her guards and said, "Go down to the camp and get me some kind of broth or thin soup. Quickly!"

He hesitated a moment; after all, it was his job to guard her, but she gave him a stern look and he went off. While he was gone she did what she could to make Wissagebreht comfortable. She spread another cloak on the ground to put him on. Then she wrapped it over him. In the meantime, she heard the sound of the battle beginning. But she was too preoccupied to do more than glance down every so often.

Wissagebreht seemed to be in the same state as he had been after he had cast that last spell on the outskirts of Lothbosc. He was breathing, but he was very weak. Having gone through this once before, Carla was not overly concerned. But it still did not feel good to see him in such condition.

At last the guard came back with a small bowl of broth. With Wissagebreht's head propped in her lap, Carla began to feed him. It was almost as if his body, though unconscious, knew what it had to do. For though he never seemed quite to regain consciousness, he did sip at the soup every time she put it to his mouth.

Down the slope, the battle was still raging. Nechtgang had been first to send in his horsemen. He used about half of all he had in a long, thin rank with which he hoped to ride right over the infantry. Unfortunately for him the infantry were steady. Even though they were pushed back, they did not break. In fact, when Bruderic sent in a part of his own cavalry to support that line, they very nearly broke through in their turn.

Nechtgang was then forced to use much of the remainder of his horsemen just to shore up his own line. Bruderic, with great care, sent his horsemen only to those places where it was desperately needed. Or, where there seemed a possibility for them to break through.

Nechtgang himself finally brought the last of his calvary in a final attempt to break the line. He very nearly did so, driving them back until they were near Carla's hill. Just a little beyond the distance where Carla could sling a fair-sized stone. At that point they began to slow. Just then Bruderic, with Lungand beside him, made the last charge. If this did not end the battle immediately it might well last for a long while. Until one side or the other was too weary to go on.

This last was something Carla knew from the talk of the leaders the night before the battle. If it came to this, it was hoped that Bruderic's men would be able to last the longer, but that was in no way certain.

Wissagebreht had come to the point where he was no longer eating. In any case, there were no more than a couple of mouthfuls of the broth left. Carla made him as comfortable as she could, putting one of his own old leather bags under his head for a pillow. Then she stood up. Her own horse, who had stood by patiently all this time, moved over beside her and she put an arm on its shoulder.

Down below, the battle was swinging in Bruderic's favour. Bit by bit, his last charge was driving the enemy back. Though there was one small knot which was holding stubbornly. It was a little swirling fight now some distance behind the main battle. It was in that fight that she saw Bruderic himself, with his uncle beside him, along with a small number of their horsemen.

Then suddenly, so suddenly that Carla never even saw the blow that caused it, Bruderic's horse went down, and he was pinned underneath. Carla watched for him to pull himself free, but he did not seem to be moving. The little knot of fighting was moving a little away from him, but Lungand, seeing his plight, held back. A moment later four of Nechtgang's men came galloping back out of that main fight toward them.

Lungand, realizing that horses' hooves, could be just as dangerous to Bruderic as any sword or lance, jumped nimbly out of the saddle to stand over the King. The Chamberlain knelt briefly beside his nephew. Then standing again, he shrugged loose his shield from his left arm and dropped it on the fallen King. He turned to face the enemy armed only with his sword.

Carla turned her face away, looking toward her horse. A moment later she dug her hand into the saddlebag, encountering what she knew to be there. Her sling and the bag of stones. The thought had never crossed her mind that she would use them again. But neither had she thought of disposing of them.

She hauled herself into the saddle and took up the reins. One of the guards looked up looked up abruptly. "Milady, what are you doing?"

"Doing? Why, I am going to the King!"

She urged the horse into motion, slapped the guard's reaching hand away from the reins, and was off, leaving the guard shouting behind her some foolishness about the danger.

She had no intention of riding into the battle, for she had neither armour nor sword. Nor did she know how to use a sword even had she possessed one. She stopped when she had reached the proper distance. Then she brought out her sling and a stone, and a moment later sent the stone flying. It hit one of the mounted men in the temple, and though he was wearing a helmet, he fell limply from the saddle.

The four of Nechtgang's men in the fight had somehow become six; though she had not seen the others approach. She picked another stone. As she swung the sling, she saw vaguely through the dust and the trampling horses that Lungand was still fighting over his fallen nephew. his mail now rent and bloody. Her stone this time took one of the attackers full in the face, and he also fell. None of them had yet noticed her, so she prepared to sling another stone.

Again it went straight and true. At that moment her bodyguards were racing past her into the fight. Now there were another three of Bruderic's men come from the main fight. She hadn't seen them come either. It was then she realized that she had been concentrating so narrowly on the small fight in front of her that she knew nothing of what else might be going on.

Then, between the time she had loosed one stone and bent to take up another, the battle was over. The King's men were dismounting to look to Bruderic, and to Lungand who had collapsed on top of him.

Carla urged her horse toward them, noticing as well that the main battle also seemed to be over. Nechtgang's men, more and more, were deserting the fight to seek safety. The battle suddenly changed into a mass of men streaming away from the field with another mass pursuing them.

She pushed her horse into the crowd surrounding Bruderic and Lungand. She barely noticed the surprised looks given her by the soldiers. They had rolled Lungand away, and he was clearly dead. Bruderic looked to be in a bad way as well, but she could see that he still breathed. One of his legs was trapped beneath the dead horse. Already some of the soldiers were preparing to try to lift the carcass to slide him out.

This they managed by heaving the carcass up with spear-shafts used as levers, then propping up the carcass with stones, until they could slide his leg out. Carla waited until that was done before she pushed herself in close enough to see him well. All the soldiers knew her reputation as a healer, so none thought to prevent her from getting to him.

It was soon apparent that the worst thing wrong with him was that he had taken a severe bump on the head when his horse fell. But he seemed not to have suffered any other damage. Carla looked up into all the worried faces around her. She suddenly realized that she had not been the only one concerned for Bruderic. She nodded. "He will be well enough. Let us move him to the camp."

Grinhalt took rapid charge of affairs. Soon two litters were made of spear-shafts and cloaks. Lungand was laid on one and Bruderic on the other, and they were taken back to camp. The first reaction of those in the camp was woe, for they were certain that the King had been killed. Grinhalt took control of that as well. He began sending people to spread the word that the King was wounded, but not killed.

On Carl's insistence, he also sent men back to pick up Wissagebreht and bring him to the camp. The wounded were already being gathered. Carla knew that whatever she would prefer to do, she had a duty to do what she could for them. She gave strict instructions as to how Bruderic and Wissagebreht should be cared for. Then went off to find the other healers.

The next morning Carla went again to the tents sheltering the wounded. She did all she could to help the healers. Then she went to see to Wissagebreht. By now he was awake and striving to get up. "I understand we won the battle," he said, looking at her closely.

"Yes, we did."

"And I have also heard a strange story about the King, and about you riding into battle to save him."

She let herself smile a bit. "It was not quite like that. His horse fell on him, and he had only Lungand to protect him. So I rode closer and used my sling to help."

Wissagebreht nodded. "And how is Bruderic?"

"Very well, though still a little stunned. He recognized me this morning, but that was all."

"And Lungand is dead?"

"Yes."

Wissagebreht looked grim, then relaxed a trifle. "Well, at least that will put to rest the rumours about Lungand having plans to eventually do away with Bruderic. Is there any word about Nechtgang?"

"I haven't heard any, but I have been working with the wounded. I have heard, though, that several of Nechtgang's prime supporters have sent people in to find out what sort of treatment they can expect if they come to the King."

The Wizard nodded his head. "Yes, I suppose that would be the next thing to happen. And now Nechtgang's support will fall away. And fall away, leaving him at last wandering the wild parts of the Kingdom with a few men at his back. Little better than an outlaw. Or perhaps one of his supporters will believe that he will get better treatment if he brings Nechtgang's head with him."

They remained silent for a little while, then Carla said, "Well, I will leave you to your rest, now. There are things to be done."

As she walked away, Carla began to realize how much she had changed over the last months. Here she was, calmly taking on the duties of a healer. Instructing people as Wissagebreht had instructed her over the years. She did so as though it were completely natural.

She was resting that afternoon when a messenger brought word that the King would like to speak to her. Bruderic was resting in front of his tent, his leg propped up on a footstool in front of him. The leg had not been broken, but it was badly bruised, and he had difficulty walking. When Carla approached, he made a sign to Hergard, who gathered up all the others who were standing around and herded them away. While the King had been incapacitated Hergard had been acting as Chamberlain. Though all his decisions had been made 'subject to the approval of the King.'

A chair had been set out for Carla, and she sat down. When they were at last alone Bruderic looked over at her. "I am told that you came to my rescue with your sling."

"They exaggerate. I did use my sling, but only until your men regained control of the situation."

He nodded. "Even so, it makes what I am about to say to you a little more difficult. Carla, I want you to marry me. There will be those who will say that I do this out of gratitude for your saving me. But I can tell you it is because I have come to know and appreciate you over the time we've spent together."

Carla sat still. It was not a complete surprise, for it was impossible to ignore the way Bruderic had been looking at her since the night they had dined in Drefcwed.

On the other hand, she had not expected him to ask so soon.

Bruderic smiled. "You are shocked? I doubt you could be surprised, we having lived so close together for quite some time now."

"I suppose I ought not to be surprised, but I must admit to being taken off-guard. Will you permit me to give you my answer a little later?"

"Certainly. Take some time, talk to Wissagebreht, give me an answer when you have made your decision. Now I must talk to my Lords."

She began to get up, but he waved her back into her seat. "Stay here with me. It will do no harm for you to hear what I must say to them."

He rang a small bell, and immediately a young page approached. "Ask the Lords to gather here, please. I have things to say to them."

"At once, Milord King."

Shortly all the various Lords were gathering before the King. Some came promptly, as though to impress the King with their diligence and obedience. Some came more slowly, as though to demonstrate to the King that though he was their Lord. He was not that much above them.

When they were all at last gathered, Bruderic spoke to them. "Well, my Lords, I doubt now that there will be any who deny that I am right in taking the rule into my own hands at this time.

"My late uncle Lungand set me up in the place of his dead brother. He was hoping thereby to halt, or at least lessen, the round of civil wars that had been taking place. With various Lords attempting to set themselves up as King. I know that there were indeed many who believed that his intent was only to knit the Kingdom together until some time when it would be convenient for me to die. And at that time he would himself step forward.

"After yesterday, however, I think there will be few who say that any longer.

"But as I have said, at this time I will begin to take the rule of the Kingdom into my own hands, rather than being ruled by advisors. This does not mean that I will take no advice from my Lords, only that the decisions will be mine.

"In this regard, I wish to ask my Lord Hergard if he will consent to serve as my Chamberlain."

Hergard stood forth and assented readily enough, then Bruderic spoke again. "My Lord Hergard and I shall confer further, and decide what further changes shall be made in the Kingdom. With all that said, what else needs to be discussed?"

There was silence for some time as the various Lords considered what they wished to speak to the King about. Many of them were now uncertain as to whether their matter was important enough to take up the King's time. While others had originally hoped to be able to dominate the King's time. But after seeing and hearing the King in action, were no longer sure of themselves.

At last Hergard spoke. "Milord, Lord Halthorp has died on the battlefield. As you know, his holding is the Berkweg, which protects us against the goblins of the mountains. He has no heirs, and it is necessary to place someone there without delay."

The King nodded. "Have you someone to put forward for this position?"

Carla stopped listening carefully and let her thoughts go wandering. At first there were such things as making the borders safe from the goblins or from the peoples of the wild. But as it went on people became a little bolder. Some of the Lords who were hoping to extend their holdings at the expense of Lords who had followed Nechtgang began to put their cases.

After a few of these, Bruderic held up his hand. "My Lords, there are some things which must be decided immediately and other things which require some thought. What you are asking now requires that there be trials and finding of facts, which is not to be undertaken in a few moments on the night following a battle. Such questions will be dealt with, and dealt with at the proper time.

"So if there are no other important matters to be discussed, let me bid you good night."

The gathering of the Lords dispersed, some going less willingly than others, and at last Carla and Bruderic were left alone again.

Servants shortly brought them dinner, and they ate together. They were talking about a number of things. All the while carefully trying to avoid anything which would bring to mind Bruderic's marriage proposal.

When they were done, she excused herself and went to look for Wissagebreht. She found that he had insisted on leaving his bed and going to help with the wounded. Though by that time there was little more to be done for them. Save for a few cases where the original treatment wasn't working. She caught up with him as he was leaving one of the hospital tents.

As they walked back to his quarters, she told him what had happened, and noticed that he did not seem at all surprised. She looked at him closely. "You were expecting this?"

He smiled slightly. "No, not entirely. On the other hand, I am not surprised, not since the night in Drefcwed."

"But what should I do?"

"Aye!" He hesitated. "Carla, I am afraid that this is a decision you will have to make for yourself. You now know more about who you are than you did some weeks ago, and you are much better able to say what you want to do."

"But I don't know what I should do! I've found out who I am, but all that has done is give me a lot of things I feel I should do! And now there is this!"

"All these things you feel you must do, is it necessary to do them all at one time?"

That stopped her, and as she thought about it, it became much clearer. "Yes, I see what you mean. Thank you, Wissagebreht," She looked at him again, "Oh, Wissagebreht, thank you for everything! I'm sure it must not have been easy taking care of a baby, and bringing up a little girl. Keeping her safe from people who might possibly do her harm. Oh, I could go on forever about what you have done, but thank you!"

It was the first time she ever saw him at a loss. It was as though he had never thought about it from her point of view. "Well," he said, "at least it won't be necessary for you to live in a draughty shack any more."

"Nor you either. You are going to return to the palace with Bruderic?"

"If he asks me to. "

"I think he will."

"Perhaps."

"Well, I won't keep you from your rest any longer. Good night, Wissagebreht."

"Good night to you, Carla."

As she was returning to her own tent, Carla heard a familiar voice call her. "Milady Carla!"

She turned. "Gadmot? Why so formal?"

He smiled briefly. "I heard about you riding into battle to rescue the King yesterday."

"Oh, the story keeps growing. I didn't ride into battle, only close enough to throw rocks until men could come to help Lungand."

He shrugged his elegant shrug. "Never fear, the story will eventually have you fighting hand-to-hand with twenty armed men. But however it was, it changes matters. I had once thought to ask you to be my wife, but I see now that would not be possible."

She forced herself to smile. "Probably not."

"No," he said, "But I hope we can remain friends."

"And whyever not?"

"Whyever not indeed? But you look as though you have had a tiring day, so I will take up no more of your time. Good night, Carla."

"Good night, Gadmot."

She had not had time to tell him that she had by no means decided to marry Bruderic. But then she had no desire at all to marry Gadmot. He was nice enough, amusing, but she felt nothing but friendship towards him.

She was sure that she would have difficulty going to sleep, but in fact she had none. In the morning, almost as though it had come to her in her sleep, she knew what to say to Bruderic. It was easy enough to find him. With his leg still lame, he was not able to move far or fast, and he had taken up a seat again in front of his tent. Hergard was questioning those who wished to see the King, and weeding out those who did not really need to see him. He had apparently been given instructions regarding Carla. For when she saw that the King was busy and was about to leave again, Hergard sent a page to summon her back.

Very shortly, indeed, more quickly than she wished, Carla was alone with Bruderic. When she saw his expression, she knew that he must be reading her own face, so she spoke quickly.

"Bruderic, I can't marry you yet. Now hush, and let me explain. You see, for a long time I only knew that I was Carla, ward to Wissagebreht, and had no idea who my parents were. Now I know, and I feel that there are things I have to do before I step into anything like a marriage. I want to know something about my mother's people. I intend to go back to the Elves, to take up the invitation of Queen Serenglas, to live with them a while.

"But if you come to the edge of the Wood of the Elves in the spring, Bruderic, I will give you my final answer then."

EPILOGUE

In the spring of the year, King Bruderic overrode the protests of his Lords and went to the Wood of the Elves.

They encamped there for three days. Finally, on the morning of the third day, a young woman appeared outside their camp. She stood with one arm thrown over the shoulders of a unicorn, and she was clearly one of the Elves.

Bruderic looked at her and said "Carla?" Then again, with a different emphasis "Carla!"

"Bruderic! So you did come!"

"How could I not? And what do you say to my proposal now?"

She smiled. "I am here, am I not?"

EPILOGUE Part 2

The Second Epilogue

The Wedding

Everyone gathered at the castle of Vorholm. It was a beautiful summer day. It was as though the sun shone down on the couple on their special day. The unicorns were dancing at the front of the hall with Quickfoot in the lead. Bruderic stood on the dais and overlooked his court. Young elves and human girls entered and began tossing rose petals from baskets they carried. Once the girls made their way to the front of the court, they were dismissed to their seats at the front where they were carefully watched by nursemaids. Then two pairs of ladies in waiting walked to the front of the court, side by side, one elf and one human to represent the union of the two courts. They then took their seats with the flower girls. Finally, Wissagebreht and Carla entered the court from the main entrance and paraded slowly towards the throne. As they approached King Bruderic, he said to Wissagebreht, "Are you, Wizard Wissagebreht, here to present your ward Carla to be wed?"

Wissagebreht then responded,"I, Wizard Wissagebreht am here to solemnly present my Ward Carla of Vorholm, daughter of Calongwir and Driwhelm to be wed"

Bruderic then turned to Carla, "Do you, Carla of Vorholm consent to be my wife and queen so long do you draw breath?"

Carla looked into Bruderic's eyes with an intensity that almost took him back, "I Carla of Vorholm, daughter of Calongwir and Driwhelm consent to be your wife and queen so long as I draw breath."

"Will you rule by my side and oversee our kingdom in my stead?"
"I will"

"Will you uphold the laws of this kingdom and enact them as Queen of Vorholm?"

"I will"

Wissagebreht then took out a seed from his robe. He held it outstretched in his hands and said, "May your love grow as does this seed. May the foundations of your relationship reach as long as the roots of this tree."

Bruderic and Carla took hands, interlocked their fingers and Wissagebreht dropped the seed into their connected hands.

They then planted the seed in the forest that night after the festivities were over.

But there was a shadow hanging just outside of the city. Hearing of the wedding, he snorted, threw some powder to the ground, and then disappeared in a small billow of putrid, dark purple smoke.

Afterword

Thank you for reading, I hope you enjoyed the story.
If you did, please check out Railroad Rising available in many E-Book formats.

And for regular updates on upcoming books please sign up to the JP Wagner newsletter at www.revjpwagner.com

Made in the USA
Monee, IL
31 July 2024

70704159-1322-47df-81be-a97367072781R01